CRITICAL ACCIDENT

The chief customs officer, itching in every finger-muscle, was just about to follow when Schickel came up to him.

"Excuse me please, your honor, you are still having mein logbook."

The customs officer nodded, still staring after the retreating backs of the Englishmen. . . . And he pulled a logbook from his pocket and handed it over without a second glance. Similarly without a second glance, the exuberant Schickel put it in his own pocket, busily touching his forelock the while. . . .

     ●   ●   ●   ●   ●

Now mark this and mark it well. The customs officer hadn't looked at the logbook and Schickel hadn't looked at it. But if this had been a film *we* should have been given a look at it. Oh yes. . . . And so would the orchestra, who would have immediately played something to underline its significance.

For it was *Dawlish's* logbook that the man had mistakenly given to Schickel. . . .

A PARAMOUNT PICTURE

STARRING (IN ALPHABETICAL ORDER)

BOURVIL
LANDO BUZZANCA
WALTER CHIARI
PETER COOK
TONY CURTIS
MIREILLE DARC
MARIE DUBOIS
GERT FROBE
SUSAN HAMPSHIRE
JACK HAWKINS
NICOLETTA MACHIAVELLI
DUDLEY MOORE
PEER SCHMIDT
ERIC SYKES
TERRY-THOMAS

ORIGINAL STORY AND SCREENPLAY BY
JACK DAVIES AND KEN ANNAKIN

PRODUCED AND DIRECTED BY KEN ANNAKIN

TECHNICOLOR ®

PANAVISION ®

Those Daring Young Men in their Jaunty Jalopies

E. W. HILDICK
BASED ON AN ORIGINAL STORY
AND THE SCREENPLAY
BY JACK DAVIES AND KEN ANNAKIN

A BERKLEY MEDALLION BOOK
PUBLISHED BY
BERKLEY PUBLISHING CORPORATION

BERKLEY MEDALLION EDITION, JUNE, 1969

BERKLEY MEDALLION BOOKS are published by
Berkley Publishing Corporation
200 Madison Avenue
New York, N. Y. 10016

BERKLEY MEDALLION BOOKS ® TM 757,375

Printed in the United States of America

THOSE DARING YOUNG MEN
IN THEIR JAUNTY JALOPIES

CHAPTER 1

*In which, retaining a careful hand on our wallets and pocketbooks, we meet Cuthbert Cecil ffinchington Ware-Armitage.**

Behold the golf course. It is very early spring, it is southern England, it is morning, and the sun is shining. The grass is freshly cut, the bunkers newly raked, the brightly colored flags recently laundered. Above them, larks are rising melodiously to a blue sky made more vivid by small white fleecy clouds. Young rabbits—yes, and old

* *Ware-Armitage*, Cuthbert Cecil ffinchington

b. Wimbledon, 1882

f. Sir Percy Ware-Armitage, Bart

m. Emily de Vere ffinchington

ed. Eton (1895), St. Godric's, Purley (1895), Rowallen's College, Sidcup (1896), Bolsover House, Inverness (1896), Granada House, Llandudno (1897), and in Australia

married. Maudie Muggeridge, 1904 (dec. 1906), Florrie Biscuit, 1906 (dec. 1908), Gertie Gunnersbury, 1909 (dec. 1913). No issue

military. Served in the Great War with Ministry of Information, San Francisco Office

address. The Towers, Stoke Oldington, Buckinghamshire; The Towers, Hicklebury, Hertfordshire; The Towers, 449 Jermyn Street, London W.1

clubs. Nil

hobbies. Golf, tennis, and draughts

ones too—prance playfully up and down the various knolls and hollows, undisturbed by the few players already out. The secretary is in his office, and all's well with the world.

Or, wait. . . .

The secretary is not exactly in his office, as a matter of fact. He is just emerging with a worried frown on his face and a telegram in his hand. And, come to think of it, there's a slight chill in the air, a certain sneakiness in the light breeze, and the centers of those fleecy clouds have a rather shop-soiled look. On the ground, too, all is not as it seems. Already the swift and slinking murderous shape of a stoat is shimmying into position near the eldest and plumpest of the elderly rabbits, and there on the eighteenth tee is Cuthbert Ware-Armitage, thoughtfully observing the movements of his partner, a retired colonel, as the latter addresses his ball.

Cuthbert Cecil ffinchington Ware-Armitage is, at first glance, a splendid figure of a man. Tall (when he cares to raise his head from its customary vulturelike niche between his shoulders), lean (except immediately under the eyes, the jawline, and the diaphragm), and not unhandsome (in a saturnine way), he wears a moustache and outfit that strike the very keynote of fashion (and then strike it again for good measure)—the fashion, that is, of the late nineteen-twenties, which is where This is At.

But it is not what a man looks like that counts. It is what he is and what he does that matters. What Cuthbert is will be only too apparent before very long. And what he is doing, just as the colonel goes into his swing, is knocking his pipe against his heel.

An innocent act?

Listen. . . .

The heel is a specially fitted one, filched from the

dressing room of a tap dancer. The pipe is custom-built, made from fine old castanet wood. And if the colonel's backside had been an oak stump and the rapping the result of a woodpecker's beak, lustily applied, the result couldn't have been more spectacular.

With a yelp, with a curse, with a *woosh*, with a roar, the swing is muffed, the ball is sliced, and a good two pounds of the finest downland turf goes flying toward the eighteenth hole. Indeed, some of it might even make the green itself, but this is small solace to the colonel, who knows that it is the position of the ball that counts, and nothing else.

And you must know that there is a small but not insignificant sum of money on this match. . . .

Cuthbert speaks. In a voice like a fine spray of diluted golden syrup and with a smile reminiscent of the keyboard of a boudoir baby-grand piano, he says:

"Oh, bad luck, sir!"

But the colonel is neither soothed nor amused. Not until Cuthbert slices his ball into the rough through sheer overeagerness are the colonel's ruffled spirits in any way calmed. And even then, thanks to a fit of cacophonic coughing on Cuthbert's part—timed to the split second —the old warrior contrives only to slice his own ball into the long rye too.

So there they are: the colonel stooping and grunting, searching for his ball, and Ware-Armitage stooping and grunting and waiting for his chance to take from his pocket a substitute ball, secreted against this very emergency, and drop it on the nearest favorable spot. In fact he is just about to do this, screening the movement from the colonel by turning his back, when the voice of the secretary calls his name.

There is an edge to that voice.

"I have a perfectly reasonable explanation," begins Ware-Armitage, spinning around to see the secretary exchanging grave nods with the colonel over in that neck of the rough. "I can assure you that your suspicions are not only unfounded but downright—"

"My dear chap," murmurs the secretary, taking off his cap and walking toward Ware-Armitage, "I'm afraid I'm the bearer of very sad news."

"Very," mumbles the colonel, taking off his cap too, with the hangdog look of one who has just been wishing an overtaking motorist in trouble only to find him at the next bend frying under the wreck of his car.

"Your father* . . . Sir Percy . . ." The secretary clears his throat and lowers his eyes. "Killed, I'm afraid. . . . Accident. . . ."

And now Cuthbert Ware-Armitage shows just how fitted he is to wear the mantle that Fate has so suddenly flung across his shoulders.

A tremor? A fig!

Ware-Armitage, Sir Percy, Bart (Chairman, Armitage Motor Company Ltd.)

b. Stoke Oldington, 1856

f. Arthur Anstruther Ware-Armitage, Bart (Changed name by deed poll from Herman Speidleplatz)

m. Alice Margaret Pettigrew

ed.   Eton, Trinity College, Cambridge

married. Emily de Vere ffinchington, s.l, d.l.

address. The Towers, Stoke Oldington, Buckinghamshire

clubs.   Stoke Oldington Croquet Club (Hon. President)

hobbies. Flying, motoring, and cards

Note: Sir Percy, a keen "sportsman," first came into the public eye when he entered the 1910 London/Paris Air Race and came within an ace of winning it. He also "won" the Monte Carlo Rally some years later, but was asked to return the trophy because, as he later explained, of French jealousy over a British victory.

A tear? A toss!

A sigh? No more than the faintest of burps.

The fleetingest shadow of a regret, then? Who do you think this is: Little Orphan Annie?

"Crashed in his flying machine, I suppose," is all Cuthbert says at first—and that none too reverently.

The others nod.

Cuthbert nods back.

But even the hardest of veneers can suffer a hairline crack when what is beneath it undergoes severe strain. Cuthbert has just remembered the five crisp pounds sterling almost within his grasp, recalling at the same time the absurd soft-centered convention that insists on the abandonment of sporting contests at times of great personal bereavement.

He lets his voice break a little.

"I kept telling him to buy a new one, but he was always too damn mean. Still, that was the way he wanted to go. . . ."

Between sheer callousness and the British brand of Manliness in Adversity the normal observer can detect little difference. The colonel and the secretary are *very* normal. So they murmur sympathetically, and when Cuthbert takes off his cap and holds it to his heart, saying bravely, "Would you chaps mind terribly if I had a moment alone with my thoughts?"—they fall for it completely.

They grunt, they turn, they examine the distant landscape and think of life and England, of death and rebirth and these hallowed fields and what there might be for lunch, while:

Cuthbert takes out a handkerchief, and blowing his nose loudly, steps over to the edge of the fairway and deftly drops the spare ball there.

And now he turns.

"Well," he says brightly, "shall we finish the game? I'm sure that's what the pater would have wanted."

The others stare at him.

"But—but surely, my dear f'ler, the match must be abandoned?" says the colonel.

Quality will out. And as a blackguard Cuthbert is of the first water. He even manages to look affronted, as if the colonel is deliberately trying to turn the situation to his own base advantage.

"Certainly not!" he snaps. "We've got a fiver on this, remember? You'd better go on looking for your ball whilst I look for mine."

Seconds later he turns and calls gaily:

"Well, what a bit of jam! Here's my ball!"

The secretary is still on the same spot. The poor man is bemused. He is still not sure whether what he is witnessing is the reaction of a man of sterling British mettle or the cavortings of a five-layered, hobnailed, steel-tipped, first-prize heel, with diplomas of honor from International Cobblers' Exhibitions at Paris, Dublin, Brussels, and the Ohio State Fair.

Remembering the rumors and complaints that have come to his ears in the course of duty, he begins to form an opinion.

He speaks up.

"Look here, Ware-Armitage, to play golf after such a tragedy is—well, it just isn't cricket."

To which the bereaved replies, all semblance of funerary rectitude dispelled as another thought strikes him:

"It may be a tragedy for you, old fruit, but it certainly isn't one for me. I mean, I not only inherit the title and the estate but also the chairmanship of Armitage Motors. Eh? How about that? I'm going to be rich, old boy—disgustingly, appallingly, stinking rich!"

Transported, he takes a swing at the ball. It floats sweetly on to the green, across it, and into the hole.

"Oh, good show!" sings Cuthbert, flinging his club into the air. "This certainly is my lucky day!"

At precisely that moment, several hundred feet away, the stoat pounced—eyes gleaming, jaws slavering. And, also at that moment precisely, the plump prey, for no particular reason, bounced forward and into the sanctuary of a nearby warren.

If only Cuthbert had seen that little incident he might have pondered on it and, pondering, removed from his face the great wide multistoried smile.

But he didn't—which is why what happened shortly afterward came as such a shock.

CHAPTER 2

Telling of a visit to the Armitage Motors factory by the recently bereaved Sir Cuthbert Cecil ffinchington Ware-Armitage, Bart.

The sudden transition from the lush pastures of the stock-broker belt to the harsh rigors of the industrial West Riding of Yorkshire has been known to cast deep gloom over many a gently nurtured heart. Sir Cuthbert's was no exception. Indeed, the name "Upper Ossett," where the factory was situated, had been invoked many a time by the late Sir Percy in order to bring Cuthbert to heel—which it always did, but fast, coupled as it was with the threat of a spell as trainee tea-boy in the family firm's sheet-metal shop. "Upper Ossett" in fact had for Cuthbert all the grim connotations that "Outer Siberia" might have had for a Soviet contemporary.

On the day of his first visit as chairman, however, the gloom was pierced and shattered at every turn. Circumstances, he kept reminding himself buoyantly, alter cases. All around him, ever since passing through Doncaster, there had been dirt, grime, soot-laden clouds, slag heaps, black chimneys—in a word, muck. But, as many a Yorkshire tycoon of the period had had embossed on his bank paying-in slips:

Where there's muck there's money.

14

And—what was almost equally appealing to a man of Cuthbert's caliber—there were under the new dispensation, besides money, heady prospects of indulging in his second-best sport: the application of a well-polished boot to the posteriors of those in no position to answer back.

This pleasant thought had occurred to him with renewed force on entering the factory the moment he was greeted by Mr. Percy Perkins,* the company secretary. For, just as some stars of the stage and screen are said to be All Heart, so Percy might truly have been billed as All —well—that other part of the anatomy. Not that this is any indication of Percy's physique, you understand. He was in fact a born worrier, with very little excess fat anywhere on his person—and even if he'd been naturally inclined to obesity, half a lifetime spent on the Armitage payroll would have seen to it that he kept nicely in trim. No; what we mean is that Percy Albert George Perkins was a *spiritual* posterior, or—to put it another way for the ladies—an eternal doormat, an archetypal dogsbody, an everlasting dishcloth in the hands of coarse and callous humanity. And what added piquancy to the song in Cuthbert's heart that day was the fact that the poor nervous fool immediately acted as if this were to be the new

Perkins, Percy Albert George (Company Secretary)

b. Rowbotham, Yorkshire, 1881
f. Fred Perkins
m. Alice Victoria Cogswell
ed. Gawthorpe Edge Elementary, Upper Ossett Grammar School
married. Hilda Clackbury, 1904, d. 4, s. 1
military. Served in the Great War with Royal Army Pay Corps, reaching the rank of corporal
address. Mon Repos, Haworth Road, Gawthorpe Edge, Yorkshire
clubs. Upper Ossett Rotary, Gawthorpe Goats
hobbies. Billiards, hiking, and bird-watching

15

deal, the liberation, the rule of sweetness and light after medieval tyranny.

"I can't say how much we've all been looking forward to this day, Sir Cuthbert," he said.

Lesser sportsmen would have put the boot in there and then, coldly reminding the miscreant that the flowers on one's father's grave had not even started to wilt and there *he* was, doing the Highland fling. But Cuthbert was not the one to rush matters of that sort. There would be time, plenty of time. Besides, there was the state of the business to look into first: all that lovely muck, all that lovely money.

"The assembly line, Perkins," he said, getting straight to the heart of things. "You know me. Let's see how the lads on the shop floor are getting along."

What he saw and heard gladdened him even further. There was a rhythm and purpose in the way the lads were going about their tasks, and a briskness in the noise of hammering and drilling and reaming and buffing and spraying that might have put him in mind of the Buddy Rich Big Band had this been forty years later. Production most assuredly was in Full Swing.

Cuthbert couldn't restrain himself.

"By Jove, Perkins," he said, with something approaching the light of unqualified approval in his eyes, "the place has certainly brightened up since I was here last."

Perkins, caught off guard, practically purred.

"Oh, we do our best! We do our best, sir!"

"And just think—it's all mine!"

Perkins winced. He'd been hoping to cope with this one after the new chairman had been liberally plied with board-room sherry. He cleared his throat.

"Well—er—not *exactly* all yours, sir."

The next time you visit a theater that sports a couple of those Greek masks over the proscenium—the gargoyle grin of Comedy and the gargoyle grimace of Tragedy—take a quick look from left to right, from grin to grimace, and there you'll have the Two Faces of Cuthbert Ware-Armitage at that instant.

"What are you talking about?" he snarled. "Of course it's all mine!"

Perkins was no theater buff. He closed his eyes.

"Well, actually, sir, it's only *half* yours. Some time ago, when you were abroad, your dear father—er—" Perkins suddenly saw a chance to apply balm to the wounds he was about to inflict and, at the same time, make up for his earlier lapse. It was a straw. He clutched at it. "Your dear father, sir, our former dear and respected employer, the man who was like a father to so many of—"

"For God's sake, man," gasped Cuthbert, "spit it out!"

"Well—he—"

"What? *What?*"

"He suffered a loss unusual even for him."

"WHAT?!!!"

Perkins licked his lips. The sound was as the scraping of nails on sandpaper.

"I don't know the details, but—but apparently he lost half his share of the works in a game of poker."

The tragic grimace wobbled momentarily back to the comic grin.

"Just a minute," said Cuthbert, "the pater *never* lost!"

Perkins sighed.

"By default, sir. He had six cards in his hand instead of five. . . ."

Every line, every muscle, every pouch in Cuthbert's face sagged.

"How ghastly! To be caught, I mean. . . ." His features hardened. "Who was it? Who won?"

17

"A Mr. Chester Schofield,* sir—from Detroit. . . ." Perkins paused. It looked just then as if Cuthbert were about to throw up all over a passing cylinder block. The company secretary hurried on, "He's been a bit of a nuisance, if you don't mind me saying so, sir. He's practically taken over the works. Trying to inject what he calls American 'know-how.' "

Cuthbert gagged again.

"You mean he's here *now?*"

"Oh, yes! He's been here six months. Works day and night, night and day. Doesn't take a penny salary."

Cuthbert's face relaxed to grim.

"Well, that's something—as long as he's increasing the profits."

Perkins averted his eyes.

"I'm afraid there won't be any profits this year, Sir Cuthbert. Mr. Schofield's policy is one of expansion. He's invested every penny he's got in a new plant *and* raised all wages."

Sir Cuthbert was looking with new eyes at the swinging production going on all around him, and there was a glint in them.

Perkins pressed on, rubbed in.

"And now he's engaged, if you please, in redesigning your father's brain child and founder of the firm's fortunes: the Nifty Nine."

Schofield, Chester II
b. Detroit, Michigan, 1900
f. Chester Schofield I
m. Marilyn Hoosier Stuyvesant
ed. Detroit High, University of Michigan
address. 13 Rivington Street, Detroit, Michigan
hobbies. Motor racing, card manipulation, model-making
clubs. Michigan Tennis and Yachting

"Is he, by God? I think I've arrived just in time, Perkins. Where is the blighter?"

"The Planning and Design Shop, sir," said Perkins, pointing to a door.

CHAPTER 3

In which the account of Sir Cuthbert's visit to Armitage Motors is continued, with sundry interesting reflections on the traits and characteristics of the British and American peoples.

Cuthbert strode angrily toward the door, followed by Perkins. And even as he turned the handle, fresh atrocities became apparent.

Music?

A *tango?*

Was this damned American turning the place into a speakeasy?

"What's that row?" he demanded with all the fierceness of one who had absolutely nothing against soft lights and sweet music in their proper context, but everything against them when they were indulged in on his firm's time. Even his half-firm's time.

"A gramophone, sir. Another of the Yankee's ideas. He calls it Music While You Work."

"There are only certain kinds of work music helps along, Perkins, and designing motorcars isn't one of them. . . . Silly idea!"

He pushed open the door and at once recoiled.

"My God!" he gasped. "Dad's Nifty Nine. The original. Being used as a bally picnic table!"

This was true. There, on the hood of an ancient motorcar, was a half-eaten ham sandwich on a bed of broken eggshell beside a half-finished glass of milk. Cézanne himself might have seen some beauty in the arrangement. Picasso might have been moved to take it apart and reassemble it *en collage*. But to Cuthbert the original Nifty Nine was as the Ark to the Children of Israel, and he reacted accordingly—brushing the lot off with a sweep of the arm.

He glanced up at the gilt-framed photograph of the late Sir Percy, glowering from the wall behind the sacred object.

"Sorry, Dad!" he mumbled. "This won't happen again."

Coming down—or rather up—to earth again after this brief communion with the late departed, he turned and saw for the first time another car: low-slung, sporty, with lines that were hardly those of an E-type Jaguar but definitely modern for those days. It was complete in every detail except for the hood.

"Aha!" breathed Cuthbert, hunching his shoulders and clasping his hands behind his back, like a battleship commander who sights, for the first time, an enemy destroyer that has been giving more than enough trouble lately. "Mm—hmm!" he added breathily.

For there was no doubt about it. There, within spitting distance, just behind the sports car, in the act of winding up a phonograph, was the man who had to be—simply had to be—the American thorn in the Ware-Armitage flesh, the Washington to Cuthbert's George III. Brightfaced, alert in every glance he cast back at the visitor, bespectacled, eyes glowing with intelligent curiosity, with confidence, with optimism—in any other breast he might have engendered a reciprocal feeling of friendly interest. To Cuthbert, however, he was the amalgam and epitome of all the house detectives and D.A.'s assistants who'd ruined his last visit to New York with their tiresome questions. And yes! There! The blighter was at it already!

"Hi, Perky! Who's the greaseball?"

Cuthbert brushed the blushing Perkins aside and answered for himself.

"I am Cuthbert Ware-Armitage, Baronet. That means you call me Sir."

Chester (for it was he) brightened up even further. He thrust out a hand.

"Well, I'm sure glad to make your acquaintance, Sir Cutty, sir! Put it there."

Cuthbert, playing it cool, put it there.

Then leaped.

Chester had a trick buzzer in his hand.

Now, one shouldn't be misled by this. Some very brainy young Americans of that period used to go in for this sort of thing. The famous poet T. S. Eliot invariably comes to mind even now in certain London literary circles with every crack of an exploding cigar. But Cuthbert, who rarely moved in literary circles and had never heard of the famous poet and his penchant for practical jokes, was neither impressed nor amused.

"How blooming childish!" he howled when he touched down again. Then, turning to Perkins, he said, as if it were all the company secretary's fault: "This is outrageous! You're not telling me that this is my partner, Perkins, are you?"

" 'Fraid so, sir. May I introduce Mr. Chester Schofield the Second of Detroit."

"The *Second?* There aren't two of them, are there?"

Cuthbert, whose knowledge of the U.S.A. west of Manhattan's Eighth Avenue was decidedly shaky, and who was under the impression that Detroit was a suburb of

Chicago—Cuthbert was staring at Chester as if he dearly wished the young man had been detained en route by one of the Windy City's favorite sons. Like Mr. Frank Nitti, for instance, or Mr. Jake Guzik, or even Mr. Al Capone himself.

And Chester was grinning back at Cuthbert as if indeed he had been so detained, and given the blessing of those gentlemen, with the promise of their full support in all his ventures, before proceeding.

"C'm here," he said, taking Cuthbert's reluctant arm. "C'm here, Cutty baby. Relax. I've something to show you." He patted the sports car's side. "Just lookit. The Triple S. *Our* Triple S. Isn't she a honey?" His face was radiant with goodwill and optimism. "You know something, Cutty, sir? With that great sports car you and I are really going places. Zowee!"

Cuthbert shook his arm free.

"Going places? To the workhouse maybe." He turned to Perkins and waved toward the phonograph. "Do we have to have this blooming row?"

"You don't like it?" asked Chester, all friendly eagerness. "I'll fix it."

And changed the record to a Charleston.

Without bothering to hide his no-time-for-idiots attitude, Cuthbert ignored him and began to lead Perkins away.

"Now I'll tell you what to do . . ." he began.

But Chester had leaped back to his side already and was swinging him around to the sports car again.

"You're just going to love it, baby. And you know what? We're gonna call it the Triple S." He drew the letters in the air. "The Six Sylinder Special."

Sir Cuthbert was frost itself. Healthy British germ-killing frost.

"In England we spell 'cylinder' with a *C*," he hissed.

23

Chester was impervious—topped with the antifreeze of his native exuberance.

"But that's the trick, Sir Cutty baby. Spell it with an *S* —Six Sylinder Special—and it has immediate curiosity value. The big come-on."

Sir Cuthbert chose to remain where he was. He flicked a disdainful glance at the car itself.

"No self-respecting Englishman would be seen dead in that monstrosity. It looks more like an upholstered roll- erskate than a motorcar." He turned to the company sec- retary. "It's the first and last of those we make. See to it, Perkins."

He'd just reached the door when Chester caught hold of him once more.

"Keep your throttle open, partner! We're in this to- gether—fifty-fifty—remember?"

"Yes, and my fifty percent says it's got to stop."

Perkins saw a chance to ingratiate himself with the British half.

"Perhaps Mr. Schofield would like to sell you back his shares?"

Chester clapped his hands.

"Sure! They're yours for a cool half-million samolians, buddy. Or if you don't have that sort of dough, why don't we . . . Hey! Tell you what. Pick a card."

He took a pack from his pocket, flipped them open, riffled them, restacked them, did the Waterfall, the Dove- cote, and the Japanese Snowstorm, riffled and restacked them one more time, and fanned them out.

One-handed.

Perkins, mesmerized, made as if to take one, but Cuth- bert slapped his fingers. He couldn't resist having a go himself, though.

"Queen of hearts?" sang Chester. "Right!" He stacked

and plucked, eyes closed, and held one face outward. "Ace of spades?"

"By Jove!" breathed Cuthbert, warming to the fellow a little.

"All rightee!" crowed Chester. "Now why don't you and I play one game of poker. One little game. Five-card stud. Winner takes all."

Cuthbert drew back.

"What? Me play cards with *you*? I'd rather play cards with my old father."

Chester shrugged, unabashed.

"O.K., tinhorn, we'll keep things the way they are—fifty-fifty."

And in time with the Charleston record he chasséd off.

Cuthbert bit a reflective nail.

"There must," he muttered, "be some way out of this . . . this . . . this nightmare. . . ."

They say it takes the spirits of the wicked several days after death before they leave the scene of their villainies. Something to do with customs clearance, no doubt. Well, if there's any truth in it, maybe the spirit of Sir Percy was lurking about that spot. And, if it was, what better place for it than behind that uncomfortably lifelike portrait on the wall? One might almost go so far as to say that so strong was Sir Percy's presence in that place, and so fierce a view did it take of the business in hand, that it actually contrived to get over from the Other Side a discreet but peremptory cough.

At any rate, Sir Cuthbert found himself gazing up at the picture—in which Sir Percy was shown with a laurel wreath around his neck, a huge silver cup in his arms, and the following caption underneath: *Sir Percy Wins the Monte Carlo Rally*.

And as he gazed, a light broke in upon Sir Cuthbert. For the first time in the last twenty minutes he managed a smile. It was a smile that made Perkins feel rather faint, having seen it so many times, heralding so many discomforting hours, on those other lips, now forever sealed.

"Perkins," said Sir Cuthbert in the light, almost gentle tones that the company secretary also knew so well. "Tell me, Perkins, is it too late for us to enter the Monte Carlo Rally this year?"

"Er—no, sir. But we've always thought it wiser to stay out, since your father was requested to return the trophy."

"Quite so, Perkins, quite so. He was a bit careless that year. . . . Still. . . ." He began to move over to where Chester was working on the Triple S. "It was nothing to do with me."

He tapped the American on the shoulder.

"I say, Schofield, old bean, you fancy yourself a betting man, don't you? . . . Very well. I think I can find out which man and which car is best for the company's welfare. We'll enter the Monte. You drive the rollerskate and I'll drive the Nifty Nine. Winner takes all. Fair enough?"

Chester gave one of his bright nods.

"Sure! But what is this Monte? Some sort of race?"

Perkins tried to explain.

"Not exactly. It's a test of endurance, run under the strictest rules, fifteen hundred miles, over the most diabolical roads and in the most inclement weather in Europe, and finishing in Monte Carlo."

Cuthbert turned to Chester.

"Well, Schofield? Are you man enough to take me on?"

"You can bet your sweet life I am, Cutty baby! But are *you* man enough?"

"I most certainly am," said Sir Cuthbert, drawing himself up and feeling the better for it. "And so is Perkins."

Perkins blinked, his fears sneaking back.

"Me?"

"Of course! You'd like a nice trip to La Belle France, wouldn't you?"

Perkins considered.

"Well . . . yes . . . that is, if I can get permission from Mrs. Perkins."

"Leave her to me," said Cuthbert. "Well, Schofield, is it a deal?"

Chester wiped his hands on a clean oil rag.

"It's a deal, McNeil!"

He put out his hand, gripped Cuthbert's, tossed himself a salad with it, imaginary but massive, and returned it crumpled and somewhat nerveless to its owner. Visibly shaken, but pleased, Cuthbert went to the door, leaving Chester to get on with his tappet clearances or differential greasing or whatever—and taking Perkins with him.

"Do you think he's got a chance, sir?" asked the company secretary on the way out.

Sir Cuthbert gave one of his long slow smiles—rather like a piano-accordion wrapping itself around a voluptuous cadenza.

"A chance? Against a Ware-Armitage? With all this at stake? Stop being ridiculous, man, and come along to the office. I've had an idea or two already."

CHAPTER 4

A brief look at some of the other entrants, proving incidentally that perfidy is by no means confined to the Sons of Albion.

Sir Cuthbert and Chester, as we have seen, were rather late in submitting their entries for that year's Monte Carlo Rally. This was due to the special circumstances already outlined. Others, however, had been preparing for months —in some cases years—and while the joint owners of Armitage Motors are rushing in their forms it might be instructive to cast a glance over the rest of the field—or at least over a significant few among them: men and women destined to play no small part in the stirring events to come.

There were, for instance, a couple of Italians worth watching: Signors Marcello Agosti* and Angelo Pincelli.* Both were policemen—traffic cops in Rome

*Agosti, Marcello
b. Naples, 1899
f. Brigadiere Mario Agosti
m. Bona Orietta Zampina
clubs.   Member of the Rome Vigili Urbani (traffic police) for the past three years. Single, but would like dearly to get married.

*Pincelli, Angelo (Vice Brigadiere)
b. Rome, 1894
f. Giulio Pincelli

—but let it be said right out that this should not be held against them. They had recently won ten thousand lire in the Tombola Nazionale and had splurged the lot on a brand-new Lancia Spider—which in itself shows how human they really were, not using it to set up their own private security business and all—and what's more, they had also decided to take all their leave and enter the Monte. True, being point-duty specialists, neither knew how to drive before acquiring the Lancia, but Angelo had bought himself an instruction book, with the aid of which he proceeded to give new shades of meaning to the term "crash course." And what were they aiming to do if they won? Why, retire from the police, of course—which should remove from the minds of the most suspicious critic the last shreds of doubt.

Marcello and Angelo, then, can be tolerated if not passionately supported, and might even be worth a modest each-way bet.

They were also bachelors, by the way.

And Marcello at least was desperately keen to rid himself of that status.

And, due to start at the same point, in Sicily, there were these French girls in their Peugeot—Marie-Claude de Vevier,* Dominique Genet, and Pascale Audolet—all

---

m. Alida Cipriani
status. Single
clubs. Member of the Rome Vigili Urbani for the past eight years. Promoted Vice-Brigadiere (Corporal) 1924. Very ambitious for further promotion.

*de Vevier, Marie-Claude

b. Cannes, 1900
f. Dr. Marcel de Vevier
m. Dr. Elizabeth Mariannie
ed: Privately and at the Hospital des Alpes
address. 12, Rue Danielle Danois, Nice

ravishing, all broadminded (Marie-Claude being a doctor and the other two medical students), all ready for a bit of sport.

In fact, all in all Marcello and Angelo had got it made and can be safely left to take things as they come, leaving us free to turn at once with a click of the heels and a brisk salute to:

Major D. V. I. R. Dawlish† and Lieutenant C. H. B. Barrington‡ of the 16th Lancers. They too had taken special leave, journeying from their outpost up beyond the Khyber Pass to the starting point in Stockholm. And lest it should be suspected that this was rather unpatriotic of them, picking one of those beastly foreign places for the kickoff instead of healthy, bracing, clean-limbed British John o' Groats, it should be understood clearly and at once that never had two more stalwart upholders of the British Raj been known to toast the King-Emperor. It

†*Dawlish*, D. V. I. R. (Major, 16th Lancers)
b. Bombay, 1890
f. Lt. Gen. Sir Bloodwyn Dawlish, K.C.B., K.B.E., D.S.O.
m. Dorothy Frances Pitt-Rogerson
ed. Wellington and Sandhurst
married. Mary Carruthers-FitzGibbon, 2 sons
address. The Fortress, Prince Albert Terrace, Darjeeling, India
Clubs.   Army & Navy and M.C.C.
hobbies. Inventing, cricket, and motoring

‡*Barrington*, C. H. B. (Lieutenant, 16th Lancers)
b. Canterbury, 1904
f. The very Rev. Trevor Barrington, sometimes bishop of Matebeleland
m. Caroline Enid Le Peu Carstairs
ed. Wellington and Sandhurst
address. The Rectory, Polberry, Salop
clubs.   Public Schools
hobbies. Hockey, music, and the cinema

was just that Digby Dawlish was something of an inventor, and he was hoping to try out a number of his brain children on the most arduous route he could think of. So, even as Sir Cuthbert Ware-Armitage was laying a few dirty schemes with Perkins, Dawlish and Barrington were checking over the gadgets that were crammed into every available corner of the major's Lea Francis. These included—and we make no excuse for going into such detail, since every one of these contraptions was to play its part before the end of our drama—these included, we say:

> The Dawlish Extending Foglamp;
> The Dawlish Periscope for Looking Over Hillocks;
> The Dawlish Snow-Melter Attachment;
> The Dawlish Anti-Pedestrian Klaxon (a loud "Hoo-Rah!" repeated three times);
> The Dawlish Extending Snow-Stoppers;
> The Dawlish Unbreakable Tow Rope;
> The Dawlish Rocket-Pack Booster;
> The Dawlish Snow Tractor Conversion Gear (comprising caterpillar tracks and skis, for fitting to rear and front wheels respectively); and
> The Dawlish Doormat.

But no. Delete that last. We have already mentioned Kit Barrington, the major's chubby-cheeked sidekick (and -kick and -kick again). Though that in essence was what he was: a doormat, a footscraper, a pawn, a chattel, a second Perkins to Dawlish's Cuthbert, with one main difference. Dawlish never took any vindictive *pleasure* in asserting his masterhood. He was not even conscious of it. He came of a long line of Englishmen who'd been born with silver spoons in their mouths and conveniently bending bottoms at the end of their woolly bootees. So it came as naturally and unemotionally to him to put it across young Kit as it was to use the Union-Jacked and crested

31

chamberpot in his tent beyond the Khyber—an *objet de vertu* that had been presented to him by his brother cadets at Sandhurst for conspicuous gallantry on the Shove Halfpenny field. As for Kit's feelings, he hadn't any either —so let's not waste any tears on him.

Let us instead press on for the moment to another of the Stockholm starters—one who has not yet arrived there, as a matter of fact, and who is still being briefed in a secret retreat miles from anywhere. And, since there is brewing here villainy of an even darker nature than that we have already seen, let's give it the full treatment, playing it as high as the old master Dickens himself might, under similar circumstances. Such monstrous wickedness deserves nothing less. So . . .

The sun is shining on the mountains. It is shining through air clearer and purer than is ever to be found in England. It is shining upon the dark firs on the lower slopes, and upon the still face of the lake beside the Schloss. It is shining upon the Schloss itself, and upon the two hundred and thirty-five windows set in the south wall, facing the lake. It is even—for nature knows no favorites—it is even shining on the count as he crosses behind the window of the Private Library. But the sun is not shining in the heart of the count. It never has and it never will. With a snap of his fingers his Excellency Count Ilya Levinovitch* orders the curtains to be drawn.

Levinovitch, his Excellency Count Ilya
b. St. Petersburg, Russia, 1871
f. H.E. Count Ivan Levinovitch
m. The Archduchess Myra of Furtenhausenberg
ed. Imperial Military Academy
address. Unknown
hobbies. Collecting jewelry and works of art

The order is obeyed by his familiar and bodyguard, one Waleska—a Polish gentleman as fair and as cold and as murderous as the snow on the mountains across the lake. Waleska in turn clicks his fingers, and a second retainer, an individual with the face of a bloodthirsty pine marten, nods. He is standing by a magic lantern that is smoking already. He inserts a slide, projecting onto a screen the image of a portly motorist—a man with dark hair and luxuriant moustache who sits on the hood of a racing car while a South American beauty hangs a laurel wreath over his shoulders.

This causes a gasp. It comes from a fourth figure in the darkened room—a large man who has been sitting slumped in front of the screen in an attitude of abject fear. Now, for the first time, he is sitting upright, and his gasp is one of surprise rather than terror.

"But—but—"

"Yes, Herr Willi Schickel †," lisps the count. "Without the moustache and with the hair dyed, that would be you, *nyet?*"

"But—but—"

"It is in fact Horst Muller. A German sports-car enthusiast from Argentina. Very popular with the ladies."

"But it is like I am twins, your Excellency!"

"Precisely." The count's monocle gleams in the light of the lantern. The image creates colored patterns on his pearl-gray homburg, making it look like some kind of jew-

---

†*Schickel*, Willi

b. Hamburg, 1885. Parents unknown
ed. Mostly at reform schools and correction centers
address. Frankfurt Prison (for the next six years)
Note: Schickel, who operates under many aliases, is reckoned
       to be the best getaway driver in the Berlin underworld.
       Unfortunately, on his last job, a bank raid, he did not
       get away fast enough.

eled crown, of devilish design. "Precisely," he says, poking forward with the tip of his silver-knobbed cane and causing Schickel to slump shivering again. "That is why we have gone to the trouble of springing you—if that is the correct term, Waleska? . . ."

"It is, your Excellency."

"—from your prison cell in Berlin. *You,* Schickel, are the smartest getaway-car driver in the business, *nyet?*"

"But—oh, yes, your Excellency, I—"

"We have all the reports, thank you. . . . To proceed. Herr Muller here has entered a car in the Monte Carlo Rally. You, Schickel, are going to drive it."

"But will not Herr Muller object?"

The count's thin mouth—across which the bright pink of Horst Muller's fleshy throat is reflected—gives an amused twitch.

"It is unlikely. Herr Muller is at the bottom of the lake."

Waleska opens the curtains a little and jerks a thumb down below. The count clicks his fingers. Schickel begins to shake more violently than ever. And the projectionist inserts another slide.

This time it is a portrait, side and front views, of what at first appears to be a roughly dug-up potato. But as it comes into better focus it turns out to be a police photograph of a man.

"He*llo,* Otto!" cries Schickel, his expression brightening.

"You know him?" asks the count.

"Many times in prison I have met him," avers Willi.

"Your co-driver, Otto Schwartz*," says the count.

Schwartz, Otto Helmut
b. Berlin, 1890
f. Fritz Wilhelm Schwartz
m. Brunnehilde Schmidt

Next there appears on the screen a map. It shows the route from Stockholm to Monte Carlo.

"You will start with the Stockholm group," Waleska announces. "Shortly before you leave, six spare tires will be delivered to you."

With a flick of his fingers he orders another slide to appear. It is a photograph of six spare tires in a neat pile. There is a flash of silver as the count directs his cane at the fourth from the top, and a flash of gold as Waleska speaks.

"The stuff will be concealed in the fourth tire from the top."

Schickel stares.

"May I inquire what the—er—'stuff' is?"

Waleska immediately slaps him across the neck.

"Nyet!" *(Smick, smeck.)* *"Nyet!"* *(Smeck, smack.)* "Do not be so impertinent!"

He clicks his fingers over the head of the cowering Schickel, and the route map returns to the screen.

"You will pass through the customs on four occasions," he says. "Sweden, Denmark, Germany, France."

The count leans forward, tapping Schickel on the knee with his cane. It is a gentle tap, but it causes Schickel to shy violently.

"You have nothing to fear," croons the count. "The customs officers go out of their way to help rally drivers." He goes over to the window and opens the curtains. He beckons Willi over to his side. "One more thing, Schickel," he says. "You are having the reputation for fast driving as well as smart driving, *nyet?*"

Schickel shrugs modestly.

---

ed. Frau Brausberg's Kindergarten
address. Hamburg Prison
hobbies. Nil

"That is what they say, Excellency."

"Very well," murmurs the count—and the room temperature suddenly drops five centigrade degrees. "But I must remind you that the Monte Carlo Rally is not a race. You will proceed at the speed set each day by the organizers and remain as inconspicuous as possible. I suggest you arrive at the finish in, say, the twenty-sixth position. And on no account permit your photograph to be taken. Clear?"

"*Ja, ja,* Excellency! *Jawohl!* I understand. Twenty-sixth position. No photographs. . . . But . . . excuse me please, Excellency . . . what about the money?"

A thin, cold, keen-edged smile plays upon the count's lips, a smile that lesser men could have shaved themselves with.

"If you are successful, Schickel, you will live like a czar. If not . . ." He takes his monocle from his eye, breathes on the glass, and cleans it with a black-silk monogrammed handkerchief. "If you fail, you will join Herr Muller at the bottom of the lake."

CHAPTER 5

The lineup, as witnessed in a number of world centers and brought to you under the one roof by the miracle of the bioscope and various other devices.

As even any fool pedestrian will know by now, the Monte Carlo Rally has starting points in a number of places scattered about the face of Europe. And, to be frank, this poses certain problems for the novelist, no matter how great his skill. Wide canvases he can cope with—sure. Just spread them out and he will slap a little paint on here and here and over here quite merrily, so long as he knows he's going to be sticking around in each of those parts throughout the course of the narrative. But to go to all that trouble for the start of a *race,* or a *rally,* knowing he'll not be able to use any of those carefully charted streets or meticulously described buildings more than once, and—worse still—put the reader to all the trouble of getting them fixed in his mind, well, it just isn't on.

Movie writers, of course, have no such worries. Given a vast budget, a cast of thousands, and a nice wide screen at the end of it all, they are able to take such leaps and vistas in their stride. Let us then make no more bones about it. Let's imagine the start of that year's rally as it might be treated by a brilliant screenwriter. Or, better still, a couple of brilliant screenwriters. Just so long as nobody expects to be served with ice cream or popcorn halfway through. . . .

FADE IN.
EXTERIOR JOHN O' GROATS, SCOTLAND. DAY. DRIZZLE.

On a headland over the bleak Pentland Firth, the British entrants for the rally are collecting their maps and log-books and listening to a last-minute briefing from rally officials, who have set up their headquarters beside a small white lighthouse. Across the roof of the little café is written in large letters: "JOHN O' GROATS." Beneath this is a board announcing: "THE MOST NORTHERLY POINT OF THE BRITISH ISLES"

DRIVERS, CO-DRIVERS, and NAVIGATORS, muffled up in outlandish scarves, headgear, and waterproofs, mill around drinking hot toddies and exchanging banter and challenges with other competitors and the band of faithful enthusiasts who have come to see them off.

PHOTOGRAPHERS and REPORTERS hurry around looking for last-minute interviews while equipment is checked and engines examined and sealed.

CHESTER SCHOFIELD, wearing a pair of wide, wide "Oxford bags" and a long raccoon coat, pushes his way through the crowd. He looks anxiously around and then heads for a telephone booth. He goes inside.

CUTHBERT is looking off-screen toward CHESTER. He turns with a self-satisfied expression on his face to listen to the RALLY OFFICIAL, who, in deerstalker cap and cape, is briefing a group of REPORTERS standing beneath a large map of Europe.

> OFFICIAL
>
> Now, although most of you have
> done this before, let's have a
> recap. Starting points this
> year are . . . John O' Groats (he
> points to John O' Groats), that's
> us, of course . . . (he moves his
> pointer to Sweden), Stockholm, in
> Sweden . . .

CLOSE SHOT. MAP.

A fifth of the screen opens up in the top corner of the map to show the simultaneous preparation for the start taking place in Stockholm. It is snowing heavily.

> OFFICIAL
>
> Lisbon, in Portugal . . .

Another portion of the screen shows the lineup in Lisbon, under clear sunny skies beside the Tagus.

> OFFICIAL
>
> Athens, in Greece . . .

Another portion of the screen shows the lineup in Athens: twenty or so gleaming cars beside the columns of the Acropolis.

> OFFICIAL
>
> . . . and in Ragusa . . . in . . .
> er . . . where's that?

REPORTER

Sicily.

OFFICIAL

Oh, that's the fellow . . .
Sicily.

The final portion of the screen shows about thirty contestants struggling to protect their cars against the curiosity of the local peasantry.

The pictures of the other starting points DISSOLVE AWAY, leaving the clear map. The CAMERA PULLS BACK to hold the group listening.

OFFICIAL

Now, by the time they reach the
common route, at Chambéry . . .
(he touches Chambéry, near Geneva,
with his pointer) all will have
experienced similar hazards.

1st REPORTER

Any new rules or regulations this
year, sir?

OFFICIAL

No. Same as usual. Drivers will
be penalized for damage to their
cars . . . points will be deducted for
arriving at check points either too
early or too late. No spare parts,
tools, or tires other than those

carried on the vehicle will be permitted.
Engines will be sealed, and . . .

The CAMERA HOLDS on SIR CUTHBERT, who
nudges PERKINS and beckons him to follow him.

CLOSE SHOT. CHESTER IN TELEPHONE BOOTH.

The usual sunny smile has vanished from his face and he
is speaking anxiously into the phone, with many gesticu-
lations.

What had gone wrong?
What mess have the screenwriters gotten our hero
into?
Has Ware-Armitage been up to something behind our
backs?
We'd better see for ourselves, and no FADING INTO
this and DISSOLVING that . . .

The Nifty Nine, with Cuthbert at the wheel and Per-
kins beside him, drew up outside the booth just as Chester was ringing off. Cuthbert wound down the window.
"Hello, Schofield, old fruit!" He greeted the pale
American. "Anything wrong?"
Chester groaned.
"The whole kit and caboodle! Holy mackerel! You
know what happened to me? My co-driver is deathly ill.
I can't possibly take him in the car with me."
"I should think not!" Cuthbert's face slipped into an
intricate system of sympathetic folds and pouches. "What
rotten hard cheese, though! Needless to say, I didn't ex-
pect to win our wager this way, but there you are. Look,

if you'll collect your things from the factory and send me half of the shares—"

"Hold it a minute, Sir Cutty." Chester was blinking indignantly. "I didn't say I was going to pull out. . . . I'll go find someone else."

As he began to move off, Cuthbert sang out, "You're too late to register another co-driver, I'm afraid. Bad show!"

Chester shrugged.

"Well, then, just like Lindy, I'll go it alone."

"Alone?" echoed Perkins. "Over fifteen hundred miles of the worst roads in Europe? Impossible."

"Who won the war?" Chester retorted over his shoulder.

Sir Cuthbert scowled.

"We did, Schofield, and don't you forget it!"

But he was much too much of an individualist to let national feeling upset his better judgment for long, and he began to chuckle as Chester hurried toward a group of people gathered curiously around the Triple S.

Perkins was all sympathy. He didn't need to pucker his face into pouches and lines to register that feeling, either. It glowed somberly through his eyes.

"What rotten luck!" he murmured. "His driver going down like that."

Cuthbert started up the Nifty Nine, his throaty chuckle vying with the sound of the engine.

"Nothing to do with luck, old bean. Just good planning."

Perkins gaped.

"Planning? You don't mean you—"

"Of *course* I did."

Now it was Perkins' turn to go all icy. A little rugged, perhaps, and somewhat slushy at the edges, but glacial nevertheless.

"How despicable!" he said. "You realize you leave me no choice but to report this matter to the authorities?"

He started to open the door.

Cuthbert didn't bat an eyelid. In fact he made with the comedy-mask grin again.

"Hold on a mo, Perkins, you sanctimonious old fraud! You might like to report this as well."

He pulled out from the side of his seat a large pink folder.

"Just a little something I found among the dear old pater's papers."

Perkins looked puzzled, but not a whit less defiant.

"It's a dossier on you, actually," explained Cuthbert sweetly. "Compiled by the Stooldigger Detective Agency."

Perkins frowned.

"Detectives? Me?"

Cuthbert flicked an interested finger through the papers.

Perkins made a grab. Anticipated. Therefore fruitless. Even as he lunged, it was out of reach.

"Better get back in the car, Adam, old apple-fancier, before the serpent gives you a nip in the Netherlands."

As Perkins climbed back in, Cuthbert glanced through the rear window in time to see Chester settle himself behind the wheel of the Triple S. An official was approaching him, a frown on his face.

Cuthbert backed the Nifty Nine into a better monitoring position.

The official was saying: "But it's my duty to warn you, sir, that to drive in this rally on your own is absolutely out of the question."

Chester was not moved.

"Is there anything specifically in the regulations which says I can't go it alone?"

"I—I don't know. I'll have to go and look it up."

"You do that, buddy," said Chester, slipping in the clutch. "And send me a postcard to Monte Carlo."

It made bad listening for Sir Cuthbert. He tskked and tutted as if he'd got half a haddock caught in his teeth, bones and all. But he wasn't the one to be stuck for ideas for long. With a final tssk that turned into a joyful cluck, he jumped out of the car and into the telephone booth. Twenty seconds later he had been connected.

"Hello," he said, hunching his shoulders, cocking a wary eye and lowering his voice. "Cuthbert Ware-Armitage here. May I speak to Lady Elizabeth Hardwicke *? It's rather urgent. . . ."

Hardwicke, Lady Elizabeth
b. Bardsley, Yorkshire, 1903
f. Clarence, 5th Earl of Bangley
m. Diana Ware-Armitage
ed. Cheltenham Ladies College
address. Bardsley Manor, Bardsley, Yorkshire
hobbies. Hunting, shooting, fishing, and map-reading

CHAPTER 6

A glance at the Latins, followed by an interesting development in the Scandiknavery up in Stockholm.

Keen-eyed observers will have noted a certain amount of agitation in the Sicilian portion of the screenwriters' animated map a little while back. It was, however, of no great import—merely the usual fussiness with which these southern races go about things. Angelo and Marcello arrived in their Lancia with a police escort, while the French girls' Peugeot—looking rather like a sewing basket on wheels—was the cynosure of all (male) eyes among the assembled peasantry. If there's such a thing as a cynosure of tongues—of sharp, vicious, female, Sicilian tongues—they were that, too, especially when the Peugeot had a blowout as it approached the starting line and several elderly bystanders were almost crushed to death in the masculine stampede to assist. Marcello himself nearly joined in but was restrained by Angelo—the more purposeful of the two. But Marcello will have his day, to say nothing of his night, and before so very long, too, so on that hopeful note and with a twitch of the starter's flag, let us switch to Stockholm and see what was going on behind that snowstorm in the square outside the Royal Palace. . . .

45

Perhaps the most eye-catching of the cars assembled there was the Dawlish Lea Francis, plastered all over its hood with the Union Jack and bristling with the Dawlish impedimenta. The major himself, clad in a military raincoat and a bright but tasteful woollen cap, was no retiring figure, either, as he took his place in the driving seat next to the trenchcoated and solar-topeed Kit Barrington.

"Well, this is it, then, Barrington. It's synchronize the watches and over the top again, eh?"

"After those blighters in front have moved out of the way, sir—yes, indeed."

The major peered at the Mercedes ahead and the two men who were messing about near a pile of tires at the side of the car, blocking the Dawlish approach to the starting line.

One of the men was our old acquaintance Schickel—a black-haired and mustachioed Schickel who'd been got up to look like the slide of the late Herr Horst Muller in every detail save the laurel wreath and South American decor around his neck. With him was the shorter figure of Otto Schwartz, who, it will be remembered, also appeared on the silver screen at the count's sneak preview at the Schloss.

"I tell you they are here someplace," Schickel whispered to Schwartz.

"Who?" whispered Schwartz to Schickel, in rather louder tones.

"Shshsh!" Schickel whispered to Schwartz. "You know who. . . ."

And they whom Schwartz knew were indeed not far away, as the two men's surreptitious glances soon revealed.

A curtain in a window overlooking the square moved

slightly. There was a flash, as of a monocle, and a glint, as of a gold tooth.

Schickel schuddered; Schwartz schrank.

"Come on," muttered Schickel. "Let's get them loaded."

He bent to the pile of tires and (for he was no ninety-eight-pound weakling) picked them up in one embrace. Then he began to carry them to the grid at the back of the Mercedes.

But alas for Schickel, alas for Schwartz. Willi had gone no farther than three steps when what sounded like a herd of mammoths came bearing down on him.

There was no time to reflect that the mammoth was an extinct animal, even up in those beastly snowy parts. There was even less time to wonder what a mammoth—and a Swedish mammoth, at that—could be doing with a British accent. And it was out of the question to pause long enough to scrap the mammoth idea and conclude that the noise must have emanated from a stampeding horde of Rugby football enthusiasts, fresh from a British win over the Swedes and heading for the nearest bar.

No.

Willi simply dropped the tires and dove—as Chester might have said—for cover.

The tires scattered, bouncing and spinning in all directions.

And the British Lea Francis (for it was but the tones of the Dawlish Anti-Pedestrian Klaxon, impatiently sounded, that Willi had heard) sailed past.

"Schweinhund!" schrieked Schickel.

The remark did not go unnoticed.

In the Lea Francis, glances were exchanged.

"I say, sir," said Kit, "did you hear what the German chap called you?"

47

Dawlish pondered.

"*Schweinhund,* wasn't it? What's it mean?"

Kit glanced around. He noted that the nearest lady was only about sixty feet away. He further reminded himself that this was quite close to the Royal Palace, the residents in which were related to the house of Windsor. He whispered in the Dawlish ear. The major blanched.

"Good gracious! I say, I've a good mind to get out and give him a good thrashing!"

Kit knew his place and his part.

"Oh, sir, I shouldn't do that if I were you!"

"Wouldn't you?" asked Dawlish, looking somewhat relieved. "Oh, all right then. . . . I won't."

Meanwhile, Willi and Otto were busy rounding up the six tires. They were sweating with more than the muscular exertion involved, too, acutely conscious as they were of a veritable pyrotechnic display of flashes and glints in the window above. And when, despite this, Willi ventured a surreptitious testing of the weights of the tires, in an attempt to discover which was the one with the loaded innertube, it was as if lightning came sizzling from the heavens. Willi hurriedly told himself to forget the loot for the time being. He concentrated on the job in hand.

By now the Lea Francis was up at the starter's table.

"The logbook, Barrington," the major was saying. "The fellow wants to stamp it or something."

"But you have it, sir."

"No, you have it, Barrington. I distinctly remember giving it to you. I said at the time—'Barrington, if you look after the logbook, then I won't lose it.' "

Kit, ever polite, made a show of patting his pockets.

"I don't remember you saying that, sir."

"Well, you should—"

And after a bit more bone-headed British twaddle Dawlish got out of the car with that brisk got-to-do-it-all-myself long-suffering manner of his seldom-do-any-thing suffer-absolutely-nothing kind. Only to find he'd been sitting on it all the time. . . .

Then, carried on by the impetus of his show of brisk-ness, he leaped back in and drove off.

"But, sir!" shouted Kit. "They have to time-stamp the logbook!"

"Well," Dawlish shouted back, a trifle piqued, "you know where it is!"

And he slammed on the brakes and reversed at high speed—smack into the Mercedes, which was just coming up to the starter's table itself.

Schickel was out and around to Dawlish's door in a crack. In another crack the door was open, and Dawlish, gripped by the collar, out at the end of Schickel's left arm. A third and final crack was just coming up when a voice called, "Hold it!"

It was a press photographer from a certain tabloid up whose street this just was.

The effect on Schickel was electric to the tune of some fifty kilowatts.

Down was put Dawlish, off came Schickel's cap, and up in front of his face it went as he slunk back to the Mercedes.

Barrington was pleasantly surprised.

"He nipped off pretty smartly, didn't he, sir?"

Dawlish smoothed back his collar.

"I expect he saw in my eyes that I was going to give him a thrashing."

Kit stared into his eyes.

"I can't see anything there, sir."

"Well, I'm not going to give you a thrashing, am I?"

"Oh, no . . . of course not. How silly of me, sir."

With which inanity—their book having been stamped—

they were off, leaving us with no choice but to return to the rally's British leg, the calflike Chester and that corn plaster Sir Cuthbert Ware-Armitage, Knight of the (Pink and Black) Garter and Fellow of All Heels.

CHAPTER 7

Wherein we are grieved to see such wondrous fair means perverted to so foul an end: a sullied idyll of the North Yorkshire moors.

"All right, Perkins, get the shovel and start digging."

Sir Cuthbert was feeling slightly swinish. Despite the fact that he'd already laid a pretty deadly mantrap for his rival, he hated holdups—and here, on the North Yorkshire moors, with the Triple S not far behind, the Nifty Nine had struck a beauty.

It was in the shape—or, rather, the utter overwhelming soggy shapelessness—of about twenty tons of mud that recent rains had brought slurping down across the road, and the fact that it had brought to a squelching halt some half-dozen other rally cars was pale consolation to a man in Cuthbert's mood.

"Go *on,* Perkins! Fall to, man, fall to!"

Perkins fell to. Or perhaps *slithered to* would be a better term. Steadying himself on the door, he leaned inside the car and stared at his liverish lord and mean-spirited master.

"Aren't you going to help, sir?"

A foolish question. It fully deserved the answer it got.

"I'd like to, Perkins, but I don't want to get my feet wet."

Now, students of bootmanship will agree that so far the

exchange could have issued from the lips of that other English pair, Dawlish and Barrington. But here comes the difference—that little extra that puts a man like Ware-Armitage in a bracket, suitably tiled, all his own.

He had pulled out a flask and was taking a swig from it. Perkins licked a parched lip.

"Could I have a drop of that?"

"Certainly not!" snapped Cuthbert. "You're driving. I'm surprised at you, Perkins."

"But—but it's cold out here."

"Well, of course it is, man. You've got the blooming door open!"

Perkins slammed the door shut. Cuthbert nodded grimly and returned to his dialogue with the hip-shaped container. And he was just beginning to regain some of his composure when he caught a glimpse of the Triple S in the rear-view mirror.

"The crazy Yankee fool!" he gasped.

For, instead of accepting the inevitable and falling-to with a shovel, Chester had driven right off the road and was making his way along an old cart track up the side of a steep cliff.

Perhaps because the flask prevented his putting his hands together in the prescribed position, or possibly because of the nature of the contents of the flask, or more likely because he had long since had this particular line cut off for persistent nonpayment of accounts, Cuthbert's silent prayer was left unanswered. Slithering and sliding, the Triple S reached the top and began bumping its way along the edge of the crag, past the landslide.

"Come on, Perkins!" snarled Cuthbert. "Get a move on!"

And he resumed his praying.

The line that had been so dead came to brief life—no doubt tapped by a minor agent of a Power operating closer to Cuthbert's wavelength. For just then Chester's glasses fell off, and as he tried to find them with one hand and drive with the other through what now appeared to be a rough stretch on the bed of an ocean, he began to wobble along the edge of the crag. Tears of gratitude formed in the corners of Cuthbert's eyes as he watched, and a great surge of joy swelled up in his throat as, with a final wobble, the Triple S went over the edge.

But Cuthbert and the Minion of Darkness had not reckoned on sheer Yankee luck and motoring skill, on the fact that even in those days most American baby carriages came equipped with two-speed epicyclic gearboxes and six-cylinder engines. Down, shuddering in every nut and bolt, hurtled the Triple S, toward the road ahead of the landslide and the low stone wall that bounded it. And up a small ridge in front of the wall it barreled, still upright, still in one piece, *and it took that obstacle with a flying leap!*

"Blast!" screamed Cuthbert as the rival car landed with a resounding *twang* back on the road and drove on.

Now, there wasn't so much as a milligram of vindictiveness in the whole of Chester Schofield II's makeup. It was therefore pure chance and nothing else that caused him to delay pulling up for an inspection of the Triple S until he was around a bend and out of sight of Sir Cuthbert—thus depriving the baronet of a sight that would have regladdened his wicked heart.

For this is where the aforementioned mantrap was to spring into action.

Chester was just stooping to tie up a number plate that had come loose at one end, when the voice of the siren sounded.

"Rameses!" it sang, in tones of unearthly sweetness and purity. "Rameses!"

Rather surprised to hear what he took to be evidence of Egyptian nineteenth-dynasty pharaoh-worship here in rural England, Chester looked around with amiable curiosity.

Then blinked.

Then stared.

Had it been the ravishing Nefertiti herself come back to life he couldn't have been more stunned. Even Helen of Troy couldn't have produced a sharper, more delicious stabbing sensation just above the heart.

And the beauty of it was that this was better than either. The face of the fair-haired girl walking toward him over the tussocks may never have driven young high priests of the Temple of Osiris mad with forbidden desire, causing them to break their vows and be condemned to three thousand years or so of suspended animation in some cramped mummy case. Nor may it ever have launched a thousand ships. But it had turned the head of many a young curate in the diocese of York, and had opened more than its share of garden parties and village fetes.

In short, this was no shade from the antique past that would dissolve at the first attempt to nibble its ear. This was a gorgeous living twentieth-century British girl, and the fact that she was clad in the riding habit of the day —long black skirt, tailored jacket, stock, and shiny black top hat—served only to highlight rather than hide a number of other intriguing points.

At great personal sacrifice—but with a thought for possible future developments—Chester whipped off his glasses, just as she called out: "I say! You, laddie! Have you seen a chestnut gelding?"

Such a flippant retort as "No, but I've seen a willow

weeping!" never entered Chester's head. Still stunned, he boggled. There can be no other word for the desperate action of a man who has deliberately blurred the edges of so delectable a view and then tries to refocus it without artificial aid. Boggled.

"My horse," explained the girl, a trifle testily. "I know it's jolly careless of me, but I've lost it."

Chester found his voice. From the sound of it, it had been lurking somewhere around the level of his quivering knees.

"I haven't seen a horse, ma'am, miss. . . . Or a chestnut gelding," he added, striving to be helpful.

The girl clucked.

"Oh, dear! How boring! How am I ever to get home?"

He moved toward her, tripping over a rock on the way. She widened her big blue eyes and fluttered her lashes.

"Where," asked Chester, with hoarse practicality, "is home?"

She pointed over her shoulder.

"Bardsley Manor. Back there."

"Huh—how far back there?"

"No more than ten or fifteen miles."

Chester sighed. And—for this is the stuff of which young Americans like him are made—he forced himself to announce: "That's too bad, then. Normally I'd be delighted to drive you a hundred miles back there—on all the scenic routes, too—but right now I'm on my way to Monte Carlo."

The young lady frowned and immediately looked more ravishing than ever.

"Oh, dear! We don't live in that direction at all."

Chester took out his hip flask.

"Have some," he suggested.

"I don't drink, thank you."

Was there a trace of disapproval in her tone? Chester took no chances.

"Neither do I," he said, flinging the flask over his shoulder.

Just then the first of the lately mudbound cars flashed past. Chester recognized the voice of Duty when it called. He moved to the door of his car.

"Gee whizz, I'd love to help you, really I would. . . . But I'm behind time already. I'm on a rally."

The girl swallowed hard.

"I quite understand," she murmured. "Why on earth should you want to help me?"

And she smiled, and the mixture of fresh dewy innocence and breathtakingly seductive experience got through to Chester, glasses or no glasses, and turned his knees back to Jell-O.

"It's rather a pity, though," she went on, "because as an American I'm sure you'd have liked Bardsley. It's Elizabethan, you know."

Chester nodded sadly.

"That sounds absolutely terrific. . . ."

He hesitated. Then the spirits of Daniel Boone, Davy Crockett, General Custer, Judge Garth, and Alfred J. Newman called, reminding him of what he had to do.

". . . but right now I don't really have the time."

Another rally car sped past. Chester opened the door of the Triple S. The girl laid a fragrantly begloved hand on his arm, setting his nostrils aflare.

"Oh, I do understand—but it is a shame, because you should have stayed to lunch and met Grandpapa. He's a bishop, you know."

Chester shook his head. In point of fact he wasn't all that impressed, having a couple of Episcopalian great-uncle bishops of his own and a cousin of rare ecclesiastical

promise in postgraduate school at Bexley. But, polite as
ever, he evinced a qualified enthusiasm.

"Terrific, truly—but I gotta keep going. Thataway!"

Another car sped past.

The girl removed her gently restraining hand. Another
waft of perfume made his head reel.

"Of course." She shrugged. "Never mind, then. . . .
I'll walk back. . . . If I *can* walk fifteen miles. Cheery-
bye!"

She started off down the road. After about five paces a
pronounced limp became evident.

Chester's mind was in a turmoil. Yet another car sped
by.

"Wait!" he cried. "Your madamship, please hold it a
second . . . I'll tell you what I could do . . . I could
take you on to the next town, and maybe from there you
can get a lift back. . . ."

On the third of the first of those sets of pips she had
turned. On the third pip of the second set she was halfway back. And on the fourth of the third she was by his
side again.

"That's awfully kind of you," she gasped gaily. "And
certainly better than nothing."

Chester jumped into the driver's seat.

"Well?" he asked, seeing her still standing at the other
side. "What are you waiting for? Jump in!"

Her blue eyes widened.

"By myself?"

Suddenly realizing that he had a daughter of the British
landed gentry on his hands, Chester leaped out, hurried
around, and opened the door for her. Giving his steadying hand a squeeze that sent shivers through his system,
she got in and thanked him.

At that precise moment the Nifty Nine raced past.

Chester scurried back and settled in the driver's seat,

screwing his eyes up in an attempt to see the road. It was no use. He took out his glasses and tried holding them like a lorgnette and peeking through one lens. That was no use, either. So, putting them on properly, he announced: "We Americans use these instead of goggles" —and speeded off.

Now before anyone starts rejoicing at Chester's good fortune in lighting on such a companion, even for what looked like being so short a spell, let us fly ahead awhile and rejoin the Nifty Nine. For there exactly the same foolish mistake was being made by Perkins.

"Chester Schofield's got himself a right bit of fluff."

Cuthbert's accordion smile stretched itself out—lazily, playfully, happily.

"A bit of *trouble* would be a better description."

Perkins frowned, puzzled.

"You see," continued Cuthbert blissfully, "unless my eyes deceived me, she looked uncommonly like a young female cousin of mine who lives in these parts. Lady Elizabeth Hardwicke. . . ."

It is a name that will not have been lost on the attentive reader.

And while we are asking ourselves what a nice girl like Betty Hardwicke can be doing in cahoots with a scab like Ware-Armitage—blood relationship notwithstanding—let us hurry back to the Triple S and keep an eye on things there.

She is studying a map spread over her knees. Chester is

singing—completely in tune with the world if not with the phonograph on the back seat.

"If you're aiming for London, you should have turned left at the last corner," she reproves him.

He looks back, then has to swerve suddenly to avoid ending up as beefburger filling between two other cars.

"Wow!" he cries, but blithely, supremely confidently. "There goes the phonograph record."

Betty gives him an admiring glance as he stretches back and takes off the pickup arm.

"Good!" she says. "Maybe now you can concentrate on your driving." She turns back to the map. "This road takes us to Harrogate."

"How come you're so good at reading maps?"

"In the Guides," says Betty promptly and proudly—then bites her lip at a thought that suddenly darkens her mind. "You know—the Girl Scouts. I—I got a badge for map-reading."

Ah, Betty, Betty! Ah, Elizabeth, Lady Hardwicke, daughter of Clarence, Fifth Earl of Bangley, and of the peerless Diana, born a Ware-Armitage through no fault of her own. Did you not also in your Guiding/Scouting days have an oath to take? Did you not dedicate yourself, as you stood with fingers to your fair brow giving the honored salute, to such cherished ideals as Honesty, Fair Play, and Spotless Womanhood? Repent, Betty, ere it is too late!

But the two-timing four-flushing little chit does not hear. Instead, recovering, she is saying: "Yes, map-reading. It was the only one I ever got. . . ." Then, in a more businesslike tone: "The trouble is, if you go this way you won't be able to drop me at Knoxley station."

"Won't some other station do?" asks Chester.

"Oh, yes . . . only . . . I'm not very good at remembering stations."

"You didn't get a badge for that?"

She shakes her head.

"No—but hold on—*I* know! London! There's a station there. It's called King's Cross or Euston or something."

"London?" Chester blinked. "Won't that be taking you slightly out of your way?"

"Only one hundred and eighty-five miles," says the minx cheerfully. "But if I'm going to be late for lunch anyway. . . . Besides, I do like map-reading, and you'll never find London for yourself. . . ." She glances at him anxiously. "You don't mind my saying that, do you?"

Of course he doesn't! He's a fool. He's hooked. His middle name ought to be Simon. He shakes his silly head.

Oh, Chester, Chester! We beg you to be careful. Knowing what we do and you do not, how can we convey to you the sinister, shameful secret of your lovely passenger? Six Sylinder Special indeed! Shabby Scheming Shicanery would be a better interpretation of the Triple S just now!

CHAPTER 8

*Being, with the compliments of the management and
the executors of the late Major Dawlish, an amusing
and instructive game for two or more players.*

One of the most stupendous episodes in the annals of the
Monte Carlo Rally occurred that year, and on the first
part of the Stockholm leg. Unfortunately, although it involved the Mercedes and the Lea Francis, nothing in those
astonishing happenings is of absolute relevance to the central thread of our history—and time is short. Furthermore,
to tell it properly would be far beyond the power of the
pen alone—even this one. It would require nothing less
than a complete film company, with a matchless director,
impeccable actors, and—above all—a battalion of intrepid stunt men. Even the script would not be capable of
meeting this one—not without the matchless, impeccable,
and intrepid aforementioned.

However, it may be of some consolation for cravers after
acrobatic excitement to know that one of the many new
Dawlish inventions inspired by the experiences of the rally
at this stage was a game—an educational game—the Dawlish Rally Game. Based on that particular stretch of the
route, it is not unlike Snakes and Ladders, and for those
who feel like a little hectic recreation after all this passive
reading, who yearn for adventure and a whiff of the great
outdoors, here are its bare essentials. Any number can play,

though two is ideal. Other requirements include dice, and a small counter for each player. (Shirt buttons, beer-bottle caps, pretzels, peanuts, old-style British threepenny bits, or New York subway tokens make ideal substitutes.) Go to it, then, games buffs. Shake away, and with a bit of luck you'll be back with Betty and Chester in no time at all. . . .

Square 1.

The Lea Francis enters a winter-sports area—complete with frozen lake, bobsled run, funicular railroad, and ski slopes. *Glide on to Square 3.*

Square 2.

The Mercedes decides to keep close behind the Lea Francis and let the Britishers do the navigating. A dumb, stupid move. *Wait until you throw a 6.*

Square 3.

Barrington makes a complete mess of the navigating and misdirects Dawlish down toward the frozen lake. *Miss 2 turns.*

Square 4.

The Mercedes dumbly, stupidly keeps on following the Lea Francis, unaware of the navigational error. *Miss a turn.*

Square 5.

The track down to the lake steeper than expected. Complete failure of the Dawlish Snow-Stoppers due to bad workmanship, strikes, outside interference, and the usual teething troubles. *But skid on to 7, even so.*

Square 6.

Schickel and Schwartz realize their mistake and develop a long steep skid themselves. *On —cursing volubly in guttersnipe German—to 7 also.*

Square 7.

The Lea Francis scatters a group of dumbfounded but agile participants in a curling match. The Mercedes scatters them even further. *Throw a fit and move on to 8.*

Square 8.

The Mercedes and Lea Francis slither to a stop and nearly collide. A first-class Anglo-German ruckus ensues. *Go back to 1, and try to understand the other chap's point of view.*

Square 9.

German bully gives the Lea Francis a tremendous shove in his rage. *Give him the old spring-loaded V-sign from the hip and slide on to 11.*

Square 10.

German bully falls with a tremendous crash on the ice. *If sympathies with Schickel, miss 2 turns and commiserate. If with the British, miss 2 turns and collapse in helpless laughter.*

Square 11.

The Lea Francis tangles with the hockey teams. *A puck in the back of the neck speeds you on to 13.*

Square 12.

The Germans again. And out of control on the ice. *Fool around like a couple of Keystone Kops' cars till you throw a 6.*

Square 13.

Pursued by irate skaters, curlers, and hockey players, all armed with unerringly accurate snowballs. *On—but fast—to 15.*

Square 14.

Blast! Blast! Blast and blue blazes! Straight through a snow wall and on to the bobsled track. *Hold tight, close eyes, pray, and on to 16.*

Square 15.

Blast again, and double blue blazes! Straight through the same snow wall as 14, only farther down, and on to the bobsled track. *Forward, screaming, to next square.*

Square 16.

Sound Dawlish Klaxon, giving unwary bobsled driver a severe case of the St. Moritz. His slipstream slows you down. *Hold your breath and miss 1 turn.*

Square 17.

Mercedes careers on to nursery slope of ski run. *Bump and bounce, fuming and fretting, to 18.*

Square 18.

Mercedes gets fixed in ski tracks, slithers under ski jump, and collects a startled skier slap on the roof. *Miss 2 turns.*

Square 19.

Mercedes runs into herd of reindeer, swerves to avoid them, and ends in snowdrift with six spare tires breaking loose in all directions. *Wait until you throw six 6's.*

Square 20.

Lea Francis comes spinning off bobsled run and goes straight underneath funicular carriage. Baggage rack gets wedged in funicular guide rails. *Fly with carriage to 22.*

Square 21.

Look down from funicular, see pine-tree tops 200 feet below, have dizzy spell and a touch of the vapors. *And miss 2 turns.*

Square 22.

Funicular carriage dumps Lea

Francis on top of mountain. *Wait until you throw an 8.*

Square 23.

Bellicose reindeer hooks the spare tire over antlers. *Give chase, missing luncheon, coffee break, dinner, and 18 turns.*

Square 24.

Back in the rally. Now, refreshed, read on. . . .

CHAPTER 9

A chapter on tactics—particularly those of the delaying category—with a note on the gallantry of the French gendarmerie.

"Oh, dear, I feel it's all my fault we're so far behind!"

Lady Elizabeth Hardwicke was doing the talking. She was sitting beside Chester in the Triple S with the map spread over her knees again, but this time it was on a road in France, not far from Calais, and it was the middle of the morning.

All over Europe the pace was beginning to hot up. The Stockholm starters had now crossed over to Denmark, the Athens competitors were deep in Montenegro, the Sicilian mob were on the Italian mainland, the Lisbon crowd were passing through Spain, and the John O' Groats shower were moving toward Paris.

"I do really," said Lady Betty, giving Chester a sidelong glance.

Less amiable Americans might have said, "How right you are, lady!" or, "You sure can say that a few more times!"—but not Chester. With a blissfully happy smile on his face he merely murmured, "Not at all! Not at all!"

"I mean," pursued Betty, temporarily overcome with remorse—as well she might be, "if I hadn't persuaded you to stop for tea in Stamford and cocktails in Canterbury, we shouldn't have been so late for the Dover ferry."

"Think nothing of it. . . ."

"And if we hadn't been so late you wouldn't have had to take such an awful risk at the quay, making the car leap the gap, just as the ferry was leaving."

"It was a pleasure. . . ."

"And if you hadn't had to leap like that you wouldn't have damaged the front wheel and had to stay up all night repairing it."

"Don't give the matter another thought. . . ."

"And as if all that wasn't enough, instead of taking the first boat back to Dover, I had to insist on tagging along and having a five-course British-type breakfast first."

"Hm, well . . ."

"But I really was awfully hungry," Betty added hurriedly, at this first hint of agreement.

"That's O.K. I was hungry too. And as I said on the boat, considering you're a lady, you've been pretty useful."

Betty's face brightened.

"Oh, Chester! You're the only person who's ever told me that!"

"Anyway, if I step on the gas I can catch up with the others before we get to Paris. . . ." He tapped the speedometer. "Get a load of that. Ever travel at eighty miles an hour before?"

Betty gasped.

"Oh, no! . . . Grandpa never goes over thirty. . . . This must be a *marvelous* car. . . ."

Chester swelled visibly.

"It sure is—six cylinders, incorporating overhead cams, a double carb, and a super-special supercharger."

"It sounds like one of your wonderful American ice-cream sundaes."

"And all entirely my ideas."

She looked very impressed. And there was something about the glow in her eyes that would have suggested to even the most cynical observer that she wasn't putting it on.

"Oh, you are clever!"

Then, glancing at the map, she said with a new briskness: "First left, then straight on for thirty kilometers."

"Merci, mon navigateur!"

"Oui, mon capitaine!"

Is it—could it be—that we have been misjudging the young lady?

But we, and Chester, had better keep our eyes on the road. For suddenly, a few bends later on, they came upon a haycart on its side, with a small two-seater parked just beyond it, and a furious farmer and an irate motorist, both bent on a little summary justice, and a gendarme trying to keep them apart, and the gendarme's motorcycle at the side of the road.

And the Triple S was pushing eighty, let it be remembered.

There is nothing like a monstrous common enemy for getting neighbors to settle their little local differences. The three Frenchmen didn't have time to shake hands on it, but in complete accord and as one unit they flung themselves into the shade of the upturned cart—and not a moment too soon. Over the recent battlefield screeched the Triple S, horn blaring, past the motorcycle (which was blown over in the slipstream), and just shaving the two-seater.

Then Chester, who didn't believe in interrupting domestic arguments, kept going, trusting that the three men would be anxious to recommence where they had left off.

But whatever the farmer and the motorist felt about it,

the fuzz is the fuzz is the fuzz the world over, as Gertrude Stein might have said. . . .

"Don't look now," said Betty, "but I think that policeman is following us."

"In this baby I eat policemen for breakfast," boasted Chester.

But idly.

Several hundred feet ahead of him there was a railroad grade crossing.

And even as he was shooting his mouth off, the bar began to drop.

Chester applied his brakes.

The Triple S came to a stop, its nose just grazing the bar.

And up drifted the Law.

Chester, with the troopers of his native state much in mind at this moment, was all set to flutter his lashes and say, "What fire, officer?"

But the Gallic approach was much more pragmatic.

The gendarme's first words were, in fact: "Look what you have done to my pants!"

And, notwithstanding the presence of a lady, he turned around to show what he was getting at.

Chester responded well. Flinging his arms about and rolling his eyes to underline his sincerity, he cried: "Oh! Ah! *Eh bien! Alors! C'est terrible—mille regrets—et* all that jazz. But it's quite O.K., officer. I'm a Monte Carlo Rally driver."

The officer was glacial.

"That does not give you a license to bring death to the roads and a chill to the vital parts of a dutiful gendarme. Ech!" He took out a notebook. "You will have to be taught a hurting lesson."

Chester rolled his eyes again—this time in desperation.

"I—er—hey! Lookit!"

He produced his pack of cards, put them through a few of their swift preliminary paces, and held them out with a disarming smile.

"Pick a card, *mon capitaine*. Any card. Whichever one you pick, it's bound to be the seven of clubs."

The gendarme picked. It was the seven of clubs. Then, with a little whinny of impatience, he remembered what he was about, knocked the cards out of Chester's hands, and kicked at them as they spilled over the side of the car.

"You are not going to play games with me! Now—an explanation, if you please."

Chester swallowed.

"Yes, well—you want to know what we were doing speeding, I guess?"

"*And* assaulting the police. . . ."

"Right. And you're entitled to know, officer. No one could be more entitled. And, of course, as I'm sure you'll have gathered, we have a very good reason." He turned to Betty, not at all sure of his filibustering prowess. "Didn't we, sweetheart, huh?"

Now note this carefully. Betty did not respond at first, despite a veritable tattoo of nudges and heel taps under the outspread map. And why should she help him out, minion of Ware-Armitage that we have just cause to suspect of her of being?

The gendarme was licking his pencil. Ominously.

"And the reason was. . . ?"

"The reason, *mon colonel,* that you so rightly are interested in our divulging—and let there be no mistake about this—we do grant—and that most readily—that you're right in this matter—the reason is that we—well—we were on our way to—to. . . ."

He shot another look at Betty. It pierced her to her very heart. Must have. For, shaking off whatever evil

71

spell Ware-Armitage had cast upon her, she gave the gendarme her winsomest smile—the one that had had at least one young curate willing to leap off the great central tower of York Minster out of sheer delirium—and said: "Actually, officer, we were on our way to the hospital . . . to see my poor sister."

The glacier began to thaw at once. It grew moist about the eyes.

"Ah . . . and what is wrong with your poor sister?"

A dozen fully rounded, beautiful British, well-practiced, girlish sobs later, and the Triple S was speeding on its way to the Sacré Coeur hospital in Paris with a motorcycle escort clearing its way ahead.

Sir Cuthbert, traveling along the same road, but nearer to Paris, was having a most enjoyable ride. Well-slept, content, he was sprawling on the back seat of the Nifty Nine, cozy and warm under a fur-lined rug, eating a delicious smoked-salmon sandwich and reading from the Perkins dossier.

Suddenly he gave a series of low whistles, spattering the back of Perkins' neck with damp breadcrumbs, and he followed this with a couple of clicks of the tongue expressive of delighted disapproval.

Perkins' ears twitched alarmingly.

"Oh, do put that thing away, sir!" he pleaded. "I've broken every rule in the book for you already. Just because of a couple of minor indiscretions."

Cuthbert whistled again.

But just then the gendarme sped past, followed by the Triple S.

"Good heavens!" yelped Cuthbert. "There's Schofield! He's bought himself a police escort. The rotten cheat!"

"Yes," said Perkins, glad of the change of subject. "And he's still got that piece of fluff with him. That cousin of—"

"Never mind about that, Perkins. After him! We'll take advantage of it as well."

Cuthbert was not the only one to have this idea. Even as the Nifty Nine moved out to join the procession, other drivers were muscling in too. And by the time he reached Montmartre and was passing under the beautiful white Sacré Coeur church, the gendarme found himself at the head of a convoy of rally cars and being cheered by interested pedestrians every inch of the way—right up to the entrance of the hospital.

Then he stopped.

And Chester stopped.

And all the other rally cars stopped, blocking the street, with the Nifty Nine somewhere in the rear.

Chester helped Betty out of the car.

"You run inside and wait," he urged. "I'll get rid of the copper."

Betty did as he suggested, waving to the gendarme as she went. Chester leaned nonchalantly against the hood of the Triple S. He too gave the gendarme a grateful flip of the hand, before crossing his arms as if for a patient wait.

But now that the soothing influence of beautiful girlhood was removed, the gendarme began reverting to type. A fanfare of horns from the stationary rally cars behind helped to insert the needle of duty a little farther. With narrow eyes, he strode forward to the Triple S and slapped it on the hood. Chester started.

"What you think you're doing?" bawled the gendarme. "Move! *Allez!*"

"What about the lady?"

73

"You can come back for her. Look at the traffic behind you! *Allez!*"

The gendarme began blowing his whistle and waving his arms. Then, with the mightiest blast yet, he gave Chester a shove into the driver's seat and the Triple S a kick to speed her on her way.

The convoy began to move again. Satisfied, the gendarme remounted his motorcycle and moved off also. Where they all went we shall be seeing shortly, but there was one car whose commander decided to miss a turn.

Sir Cuthbert tapped Perkins on the shoulder.

"Let them go," he said. "Pull in here. I have to go into the hospital."

"Not feeling well, Sir Cuthbert?" asked Perkins hopefully.

"Top hole, thank you, Perkins," said Cuthbert, getting out of the car.

After a couple of steps he was back and slapping Perkins' hand as it reached toward the side pocket.

"Now, now, Perkins!" said Cuthbert. He transferred the dossier to one of his own pockets. "That's the only copy I have! We don't want to add stealing to our other misdemeanors, do we?"

Poor, poor Perkins!

But there were more urgent matters afoot, we fear.

Sir Cuthbert was already at the door of the hospital.

And Lady Betty, remember, was still somewhere inside. . . .

CHAPTER 10

A short cine-tour of Paris.

There are some scenes too sordid for even the most hard-bitten of prose writers to touch. Retiring as gracefully as possible with our forty-foot pole, then, we leave this next one to the screenwriters. . . .

HIGH SHOT. DOWN NARROW STREET. MONTMARTRE. DAY.

The TRIPLE S leads the rally cars down a narrow cobbled street. At an intersection, CHESTER makes a move to turn left, then the car skids to correct itself and turns right.

INTERIOR. TRIPLE S. TRAVELING.

CHESTER is trying to find his way out of the warren of streets, anxiously looking at the map on the seat beside him and trying vainly to pick out the correct turnings.

The motorcade comes to a hairpin corner. The TRIPLE S sweeps back left, and the other cars wildly follow suit.

INTERIOR. HOSPITAL CORRIDOR. SACRÉ COEUR.

NURSES, PATIENTS, and HOSPITAL VISITORS are passing in and out through glass-paneled swing doors. Each time the right-hand door opens SIR CUTHBERT can be seen shaking his finger, admonishing somebody (although because of the general chatter we do not hear what he says). Now a NURSE passes through the left-hand door, and as it is pushed open we see that it is BETTY that CUTHBERT is talking to. (The background music underlines the significance of this.) She is shaking her head angrily, and clearly denying some accusation. The doors close, and both are blocked out of sight for the moment. The doors open again as a stretcher is wheeled through, carrying a difficult blood-transfusion case, and now, wincing, CUTHBERT pulls out a billfold, counts out several bills, and hands them to BETTY, who thanks him and stuffs them into her jacket pocket. Is this (the screenwriters have the gall to ask) dirty work at the crossroads?

EXTERIOR. MONTMARTRE STREETS.

The TRIPLE S is leading the rally drivers in a mad ride around the houses. (UNDERCRANKED)

EXTERIOR. DEAD END.

The TRIPLE S turns into the narrowest of cobbled streets, followed by all the other cars. They come to a stop behind CHESTER at the dead end. They all jump out of their cars, maps in hand, shouting recriminations.

DRIVERS (ad lib)

—Can't you read a rhubarb map?
—You trying to ruin the rhubarb rally?
—Rhubarb amateur!

Those Daring Young Men In Their Jaunty Jalopies

(et rhubarb cetera)

CHESTER sits in his car and turns up his collar. He gives a final despairing look at the map and flings it out of the car.

The other cars back out of the street amidst cries of confusion. CHESTER slips into reverse gear and gives a cry.

> ### CHESTER
>
> Betty! (he turns to camera)
> Unfortunately *I* never got a badge
> for map-reading!

EXTERIOR. HOSPITAL. SACRÉ COEUR.

BETTY is standing at the entrance, trying not to notice several small boys kidding her about her riding habit and galloping imaginary horses around her. Suddenly she brightens as she sees the TRIPLE S approaching. CHESTER pulls up beside her.

> ### CHESTER
>
> Boy, oh boy! Am I glad to
> see you. I got lost.

> ### BETTY (happily)
>
> You can't do without me?

He shakes his head.

> ### BETTY
>
> Well, in that case I'll go all
> the way to Monte with you.

CHESTER

You will? Atta girl! Jump in!

He starts to help her inside.

CHESTER

I have to check in by noon at the
Pont Alexander III—wherever that is.

BETTY

Don't worry, I'll find it—but
(smiling sweetly) I must get a
toothbrush and a couple of
hankies on the way. I won't be a
jiff. You don't mind, do you,
Chester?

CHESTER

(opening his own door) You bet
your sweet life I don't . . .
Lady Betty. . . .

His enthusiasm causes him to pull the handle too hard,
and it comes off in his hand. He looks at it, shrugs, and
happily tosses it away.

CHECKPOINT BELOW THE PONT ALEXANDRE III. PARIS. DAY.

A small crowd of excited Parisians is gathering at the
checkpoint, where, under the usual banners and displays
of national flags, rally officials are setting up tables with
refreshments and sorting out their lists and papers.

There is a cheer as the NIFTY NINE draws up alongside the quay and stops beside the table. SIR CUTHBERT steps out. He gives a wave to the crowd and smiles superciliously at the RALLY OFFICIAL.

> CUTHBERT
>
> Cuthbert Ware-Armitage, Baronet, reporting.

The OFFICIAL looks a little surprised, but smiles.

> OFFICIAL
>
> Ah, yes, of course. May we have your logbook?

> CUTHBERT
>
> Certainly. (He snaps his fingers.) Logbook, Perkins, logbook.

PERKINS leans out of the car, taking the logbook from his breast pocket and hands it to the OFFICIAL.

The OFFICIAL time-stamps the logbook, makes an entry in it, and hands it back to CUTHBERT without comment. CUTHBERT glances at it and reacts.

> CUTHBERT
>
> What's this? *Penalty* of ten points?

> OFFICIAL
>
> You're exactly an hour early, sir. You're supposed to be exactly on time.

CUTHBERT

I trust you've given that blasted
American the same penalty!

OFFICIAL

No, sir. You're the first here.

CUTHBERT'S face darkens.

CUTHBERT

Blue blazes and blasted ding-dongs!

EXTERIOR. RUE DE LA PAIX. PARIS. DAY.

The TRIPLE S is parked outside a smart-looking shop.
CHESTER is fast asleep at the wheel. Suddenly he gives
a jerk, opens his eyes sleepily, looks around to get his
bearings, glances at his three watches, and sits up wide
awake.

CHESTER

Thomas Edison Bell! Half-past one!

He springs out of the car and rushes to the shop window.

Just above eye level is a brass rail from which hangs vel-
vet curtains. By standing on tiptoe, CHESTER can just
see over the top. He reacts as he sees:

THROUGH THE WINDOW,

BETTY standing in front of a long mirror. She is wearing

a completely new and elegant outfit, entirely suitable for a tea party at the Ritz or even Sunday brunch at the Stanhope, but absolutely useless for a rally. A dandified COUTURIER is hovering near her and presenting MODELS wearing other chic dresses. It seems the lady cannot make up her mind.

CHESTER nearly has a fit. He raps the window.

INTERIOR. COUTURIERS.

BETTY and the others stop in their tracks and look up.

CHESTER, OUTSIDE THE WINDOW, points anxiously to his wristwatch and indicates that they must go.

One of the ASSISTANTS helps BETTY into a luxurious fur coat. She takes a last glance at herself in the mirror.

> BETTY
>
> Oh, dear! I'll have to go.
> I'll take the dresses and this
> coat. Will this be enough?

She pulls out the money which Cuthbert was seen giving her at the hospital.

> BETTY
>
> If it isn't—send the bill to
> Sir Cuthbert Ware-Armitage, The
> Towers, Hicklebury, Hertfordshire.

Once again the music underlines the significance of this.

> BETTY (sweetly)
>
> . . . that's in Angleterre.

81

EXTERIOR. RUE DE LA PAIX. PARIS. DAY.

CHESTER paces outside the shop, his hands clenched behind his back.

The door opens, and BETTY appears in the dress and fur coat. She holds her forefinger to her lips contritely.

CHESTER

Two hours! What are you
trying to do to me?

BETTY

Oh, have I been naughty, Chester?
But you've had a lovely rest,
haven't you?

She takes hold of the lapel of his coat and looks into his eyes.

BETTY

And you wouldn't want me to go
all the way to Monte dressed only
in my riding habit, would you?

CHESTER gazes with adoration at this feminine vision and shakes his head.

CHESTER

Wow! You sure look great!

BETTY

Thank you. . . .
(She steps back and strikes a

pose in front of him.) Do you
think I need a hat?

CHESTER

Oh, no ... no ... no!

He bundles her into the car, closes the door, and turns.
His face falls as he sees:

Coming out of the shop, FOUR ASSISTANTS, each carrying a large cardboard box.

CHESTER

A couple of hankies and a toothbrush, huh?

Then he shakes his head in despair and opens the rear
door of the TRIPLE S. It is already well stuffed with
gear. He starts desperately to try to find room for the
boxes. THE BOXES BLACK OUT THE SCREEN.
When it clears, we see:

EXTERIOR. CUSTOMS OFFICE. FRONTIER BE-
TWEEN DENMARK AND GERMANY. DAY.

Which, as will readily be agreed, is a very smart way of
switching scenes—much to be envied by prose writers. But
it is time to return to the older medium, and the
merely orthodox villainy, skulduggery, and
criminality of Herren Schickel and
Schwartz, using for this purpose,
to show that we too are not
without a few neat

technical tricks,
this slow fade
to chapter
ending
white. . . .

CHAPTER 11

Of customs officials, their nasty suspicious minds, and their shameful treatment of an officer and gentleman.

There was hell to pop at the Danish-German frontier when the Stockholm contingent started arriving there. The German customs seemed to be in a particularly rotten frame of mind and were making competitors get out of their cars, unfasten their baggage, and open the car trunks. A rally official did his best to remonstrate.

"This is absolutely outrageous!" he said. "We've never had customs interfere with a rally before!"

The reply was dry and to the point.

"We have never before received a tipoff that one of your competitors was smuggling stolen jewelry."

"But—but it's ridiculous!" spluttered the official. "All these men are sportsmen—well-known drivers."

The chief customs officer consulted a list.

"What about Horst Muller?"

He looked up and nodded toward the Mercedes, where Schickel was standing with Schwartz. They were looking about them with blue-eyed innocence and—unfortunately for them—a marked lack of impatience by contrast with the other competitors.

The rally official snorted.

"But he's a famous German racing driver from the Argentine!"

The customs man grunted and thumbed through the sheaf of papers.

"And the driver of the car with the Union Jack? What about him?"

"Pah! He's an Indian Army officer. He's traveled ten thousand miles to take part in this rally, to show off his inventions. He's hardly likely to be a smuggler."

The customs officer's eyes narrowed.

"So. . . . He may have invented a place in which to smuggle jewels. . . . And anyway, if he is an Indian Army officer, why is his skin not dark?"

Dawlish's car was pulling alongside the Mercedes. Still smarting from their run-in on the ice back at Lake Malmö, the two crews turned their backs on each other. This—witnessed by someone who knew nothing about the feud—looked odd in itself.

The customs officer signaled to two of his assistants.

"We will search the German's car first," he said.

As one of the men held out a board for him to read, Schickel swelled with confidence.

"Nothing to declare," he said.

"Logbook?"

Schickel handed it over to the chief customs officer. Then he blinked as the man put it in his pocket and motioned to the other two to get on with the search. As they started to unstrap the six spare tires, Schickel began to sweat around the ears.

"I am telling you we have nothing to declare," he croaked. Then, attempting a little easy jocularity, he added: "Not even *ein* frankfurter!"

The chief customs officer flicked him a glance that would have sent better comedians than Willi Schickel sobbing back to their dressing rooms. Then he took out a knife and split the canvas covering of one of the tires. Having run his hand around the inside rim and so satisfied himself that there was nothing inside, he turned to the next tire and stabbed that.

Had it been the heart of Willi himself it couldn't have produced a keener look of frozen anguish on the victim's face. As for Schwartz, with tight-shut eyes and silently moving lips, he looked much as a man at the awkward end of a firing squad might look.

Dawlish and Barrington were not unwilling witnesses of this little cameo. The major's lip curled.

"Just the sort of rotter you'd expect to try to swindle the customs."

"I quite agree, sir."

"Despicable."

"Utterly, sir. . . . I say, sir—I hope they don't find our cigarettes . . ."

Dawlish gave a start.

". . . or our Scotch, sir."

The major frowned.

"Don't fuss so, Barrington. They won't search us. Any fool can see we're British."

Nevertheless, he felt moved to get out of the car and strike what he fervently hoped was a nonchalant pose, with his foot on the battery container strapped to the running board.

This was not lost on Schickel. Unable to bear the sight of the customs officer's plunging knife and questing hand, he had turned his head and in the driving mirror observed the major's action and expression. With the swiftness of his kind, he grasped this straw, and nudged the chief customs officer, and whispered in his ear, and the straw became a two-inch steel hawser.

"So. . . ." hissed the customs officer, putting down the tire he had just selected. "Ssank you. . . ."

And he moved off toward Dawlish like a large sleek cat after a bedraggled starling. One of his assistants went with him at once, while the other hurriedly made the necessary chalk marks on the rest of the Mercedes' tires and baggage. Then he too skipped off, eager to join the little throng beside the Lea Francis.

Air came out of Schwartz's lips like a slow puncture. Schickel giggled happily. The chief customs officer was already tapping Dawlish on the knee of the leg that mounted guard over the battery container, and with every tap the Englishman went more rigid.

"Logbook, sir, if you please," murmured the customs officer.

Like a voice from the Other Side at a third-rate séance, the following message came scraping from the driest of Dawlish throats:

"For our own personal use, sir, I assure you. I'm a very heavy smoker and . . . Barrington here . . . he's a very heavy drinker."

"I say, steady, sir!" protested his companion.

"For his size he is, that is," Dawlish gibbered on. "A preternaturally keen thirst, which requires . . ."

"You will both come this way," said the chief customs officer icily. "You," he said to his assistants, "will strip the car. I," he continued, nodding grimly at Dawlish and Barrington, "will strip its occupants."

"Stuh-rip us?" gasped Barrington. "Naked? In the nude?"

"That's what I said."

Dawlish stood firm, absolutely rigid.

"The only persons permitted to see me in the pink," he intoned, "are Mrs. Dawlish—that's my memsahib; Rabindranath Veeraswamy—that's my batman; and Major E. R. Crossthwaite-Ponsonby—that's my doctor. Accordingly, your request is refused. That is all I have to say."

The chief customs officer nodded to his assistants. It was nod No. 13(b) and, with typical German thoroughness, the assistants knew precisely what to do. To say that the Englishmen's feet didn't touch the ground all the way to the customs shed would be a gross exaggeration. But it was *as if* they didn't, such was the speed with which the transference was executed.

The chief customs officer, itching in every finger muscle, was just about to follow when Schickel came up to him.

"Excuse me please, your honor, you are still having *mein* logbook."

The customs officer nodded, still staring after the retreating backs of the Englishmen.

"Ah yes, of course . . . here. . . ."

And he pulled a logbook from his pocket and handed it over without a second glance. Similarly, without a second glance, the exuberant Schickel put it in his own pocket, busily touching his forelock the while.

"Danke, danke, danke, danke. . . ."

Then he hurried off back to his car, chuckling hugely.

Now, mark this, and mark it well. The customs officer hadn't looked at the logbook, and Schickel hadn't looked at it. But if this had been a film, *we* should have been given a look at it. Oh, yes. . . . And so would the orchestra, who would have immediately played something to underline its significance.

For it was *Dawlish's* logbook that the man had mistakenly given to Schickel. . . .

CHAPTER 12

In which further trouble is encountered at the cus-
toms—with some acute observations on the British
race.

The journey between Lübeck and Strasbourg is no Sun-
day-morning drive by any standards, but it was a stretch
along which both the Mercedes and the Lea Francis were
able to make up for lost time.

With Willi Schickel, of course, it was familiarity with
the terrain that lent wings to his wheels—for many had
been the times that he had sped along the roads of his Fa-
therland with anxious bank raiders crouching in the rear
seat. With Major Dawlish, on the other hand, it was the
magnificent head of indignant British steam he'd worked
up in the customs shed at Lübeck—that and the effects of
the Dawlish Patent Finger Extractor or some similar device we failed to include in the catalog earlier.

It was therefore not very far behind the rest of the
Stockholm contingent that the two cars came into view of
the long steel bridge over the Rhine.

Fast as these splendid vehicles had been able to travel,
however, and masterly though their drivers might have
been, they had been unable to outstrip the message that
had flown along the same route—not long before—by
means of that miracle of modern science and engineering,
the telephone.

The exact wording of the message has been lost to us, but here is a reliable transcript of the French customs officer's response:

"Oui, m'sieur, oui . . . Horst Muller . . . the driver from the Argentine. . . . No, he has not passed through yet. . . . *Oui,* we will search him and his car most diligently. . . . He may be in disguise? . . . *Entendu.* . . ."

With which he put down the receiver, crooked a finger, and said to the assistant who came hurrying to his side: "Horst Muller . . . find him."

So it came to pass that the assistant customs officer reacted with a start on glancing at the logbook handed to him by Kit Barrington, for it bore, as we have seen and the two Britishers had not, the legend "Horst Muller."

Dawlish had just stepped out to stretch his legs. The customs official tapped him on the shoulder.

"A moment, *m'sieur.* I have instructions to search you. Will you please step into the office."

By dint of repeating to himself the whole of Kipling's noble poem "If" every five miles along the route from Lübeck, Dawlish had just about managed to restore his British calm.

Now he exploded.

"No, I will *not!*" he howled. "I've already written to the War House about the disgusting treatment we received at the hands of you customs wallahs up in Lübeck, and if I have any trouble from you chaps I shan't hesitate to write to Mr. Clemenceau, Mr. Poincaré, or whoever else happens to be your Prime Minister this week!"

He folded his arms and stood firm.

The customs officer glanced at a colleague and nodded. It was that old 13(b) nod again, but this time in French. And this time Dawlish's feet literally didn't touch the ground on the way to the shed, for, grasping him by the elbows of his still stubbornly folded arms, and using them as if they were the handles on a large Wedgwood funerary urn, they lifted him bodily and marched him off.

Barrington, escorted by a third officer, came quietly.

Now, who should arrive at that moment—just in time to see the major and his companion enter the shed—but Schickel and Schwartz.

Schickel groaned.

"I do not like it, Otto. The customs are being far too suspicious. They are smelling rats."

He took out his logbook in readiness.

"Don't lose your nerve, Willi," murmured Otto. "This will be the last post we shall have to pass."

"I know, I know, Otto. But it is always at the last fence where we Germans are getting a kick in the rearguard!"

He glanced down at the book in his hand. Then glanced again. Then gaped.

"*Gott in Himmel,* Otto! Look! 'Major Digby Dawlish and Lieutenant Christopher Barrington'! We have been given the wrong book. Now we *are* up to our necks in *der* muddy waters!"

Otto grabbed the book and stared at it.

Then: "Wait!" he cried. "If you are having the major's papers, he must be having ours. . . . And, Willi, look. . . ."

Willi looked, and saw: the Lea Francis, surrounded by a mob of customs men, was being taken apart—bit by bit by bit. Already the Dawlish battery of inventions lay strewn around on all sides.

A slow smile spread across Schickel's face—a smile that would have been worthy of Sir Cuthbert Ware-Armitage himself.

"*Ja.* . . . So. . . ." he murmured thoughtfully. "And if they are thinking Major Dawlish is Horst Muller, then they must be thinking that Horst Muller is Major Dawlish."

He rummaged around in the back and pulled out a British society magazine he had filched from a hotel somewhere along the route. Quickly he flipped to a pageful of photographs depicting a grouse-shooting party: to foreign eyes a veritable phantasmagoria of flat caps, tweeds, monocles, and rugged pipes clenched between equally rugged teeth.

"We must be British, Otto," said Schickel, readjusting his own cap until it sat straight between his ears and over his brow. "Where is *mein* pipe?"

Thus it transpired that—while outraged whinnies floated from the customs shed—the Mercedes purred up to the barrier with a couple of the strangest, flat-capped, pipe-clenching Englishmen in the front seats that ever the officer on duty had seen—and he'd seen some beauties in his time, believe you us.

"Bung-ho!" caroled Schickel, handing him the logbook. "Here is the spiffing logbook, doncher know, pip, pip. We are having a time which is topping hole in this rally. What about a nice cup of tea and some steaming crumpets, hey, what, old pea? Three rousing cheers and God save the Kaiser!"

He raised his cap, stiff-armed. The customs officer lowered his bottom jaw. Then, words failing to skip to his service, he stamped the book and dumbly handed it back.

The Mercedes shot off.

The officer shrugged.

Then he went back to help his colleagues in their reduction of the Lea Francis to its lowest common denominator, muttering as he did so: "A strange race, the British . . . a very strange race. . . ."

CHAPTER 13

An explosive situation, in which Sir Cuthbert Ware-Armitage displays a resourcefulness that surprises even Perkins.

Talking about Sir Cuthbert and his long slow smile, what was *that* scoundrel up to by this time?

A good question, if somewhat impertinently put.

Sir Cuthbert Ware-Armitage, you must know, was proceeding in the Nifty Nine up a mountain road quite close to the Alps. And, far from being "up to" anything, he was engaged in nothing more devilish than reclining peacefully in the back seat and enjoying the view.

Admittedly, he wasn't going into ecstasies over it. He was not, for example, at one with the thinker Ruskin in subscribing to the belief that "mountains are the beginning and the end of all natural scenery." Nor did he call to mind those haunting lines of Donne's, about somebody going "o'er the white Alps alone." For one thing, he was not alone, and for another, he'd never heard of Donne, let alone the fellow's elegies. Tennyson he had heard of, certainly, and indeed had been full of admiration for the gifted lord ever since he'd heard about the old boy's sinking a pint of port every night just before going to bed. Nevertheless, Cuthbert was not sufficiently inspired just now to peer delightedly about him, tap Perkins on the shoulder, and cry: "Doesn't it remind you of those touching lines: 'I climbed the roofs at break of day; Sun-smitten Alps before me lay?' " In any case, it was sunset. A reddish-golden light was glowing softly through the light sprinkle of snowflakes that were falling on the car and the road ahead and the little filling station at the side of the——

"I say, Perkins, stop!" cried Sir Cuthbert, suddenly coming out of his reverie. "Can't you read, man?"

He pointed to a rally sign in front of the filling station. It read: LAST GASOLINE THIS SIDE OF THE ALPS. Perkins glanced at the fuel indicator, nodded, and pulled up. Cuthbert climbed out of the car. He looked around. It wasn't exactly a swinging station, even for those days. No row of pumps—indeed, no standing pump at all—let alone a team of attendants hurrying forward with windshield-cleaning equipment, free road maps, light-hearted stickers, fun badges for the kids, and Your Chance to Win a Thousand Dollars in Our Great New Contest. Just a wooden hut, about twenty fifty-gallon drums of gas lying on their sides, and an elderly peasant limping toward them from a house farther down the valley.

"Fill her up," commanded Cuthbert.

The man touched his cap and fitted a hand pump to the nearest drum. Then, as the other end of the hose was being stuffed into the Nifty Nine's tank, Cuthbert took out a cigar and placed it in his mouth.

"Mais, non, m'sieur!" cried the attendant when he heard the scratch and flare of Cuthbert's match. *"Interdit de fumer! Interdit de fumer! M'sieur,* if you *please,* no smoking!"

Cuthbert drew deep on his cigar.

"Rubbish!" he rasped. "A few sparks aren't going to set fire to this lot!"

The attendant turned appealing eyes to Perkins—only

to receive a shrug and an it's-no-use-arguing-with-this-jerk look that leaped all language barriers.

But Cuthbert did at least have the grace to turn his back and the brightly glowing end of his cigar away from the trembling peasant, and for that small act of mercy he was immediately—and some would say overprecipitately—rewarded by Providence. For now he was able to see the sign again.

Now, circumstances—as we have been at pains to point out before—alter cases. Work it out for yourself. When first seen, after a pleasant hour or so spent musing on the scenery, the words LAST GASOLINE THIS SIDE OF THE ALPS come as a practical reminder—a vaguely rude but necessary interruption to one's train of thought—and nothing else. Seen five minutes later, however, after discussing with a fainthearted and no doubt effeminate foreigner the risk of an explosion and consequent destruction of the entire stock, the whole thing takes on a new complexion.

And here the familiar long slow smile did start to spread across the Ware-Armitage face.

Quelling it, he turned and asked casually: "Am I the first of the rally drivers to pass this way?"

The man nodded.

"Oui, m'sieur."

Cuthbert watched thoughtfully as the attendant stopped pumping and screwed the cap on the Nifty Nine's gas tank, which was now overflowing. Then, after carefully selecting the largest bill he could find, Cuthbert held it out.

"You have nothing smaller, *m'sieur*?"

"Afraid not, old *garçon*."

"But I shall have to go all the way down to the house, *m'sieur*."

"Have a nice trip," said Cuthbert pleasantly.

"Perhaps the other *m'sieur* . . . ?"

But, as Cuthbert had calculated, Perkins—badly bitten by his experiences of the last few days—was not in the least inclined to volunteer anything smaller himself.

Grumbling, the attendant limped off.

"Right, Perkins," said Cuthbert, leaping back into the Nifty Nine, "off, off, and away we go!"

"But what about your change?"

"Oh, let him keep it!" said Cuthbert, a kindly smile playing on his lips. "You know by now what a generous lovable old goat I am. I simply can't resist helping lame dogs over the thingumibob, and by golly, if I can do it by stealth, by stealth it shall be done. Not a word of this to anyone, Perkins."

Perkins wondered if the fumes from the gasoline had gone to his employer's head. Wondering further if perhaps this might not be the time to put in a well-phrased plea for the return of the dossier, he did as he was bade and began to pull away.

Cuthbert meanwhile had been taking a long steady drag at the cigar. Then, as they began to move, he blew on its already brightly glowing end and tossed it out of the window toward the gasoline drums.

"Drive like a demon, Perkins!" Cuthbert urged now.

And like hell indeed it seemed just then, for, with a woosh and a flare and a tremendous bang, one of the drums exploded.

"Too bad about the other competitors!" chortled Cuthbert. "If they run out of gas, I mean!"

Then Perkins saw it all.

Shocked, he slammed on the brakes, just in time to see another drum go up. He jumped out of the car, but then stood where he was when he saw that there was nothing he could do to save the filling station. Cuthbert got out and stood beside him. His face glowed with more than the reflected flames.

"What a rotten filthy trick!" gasped Perkins, wondering if there were no limits to the depths of his employer's iniquity. "You did that on purpose!"

Cuthbert had the cheek to look hurt.

"Oh, come now, Perkins, come now! You've got a rotten twisted mind, that's your trouble, laddie. It was clearly an accident. It—it—"

Horror had suddenly replaced the look of pain and gentle reproach.

"My God!" he cried, pointing.

And well he might. The overflowing tank of the Nifty Nine had left behind it a narrow train of gasoline, and along that train, rapidly gaining on them, there approached a sprightly flickering flame, getting bigger with every inch.

Cuthbert made a move as if to go and stamp it out, then changed his mind. Grabbing his bag instead, he ran off into the snow. Perkins was in no mood for heroics either. Grabbing his own bag, he followed, flinging himself down beside Cuthbert just in time. With the biggest explosion yet, up went the Nifty Nine's fuel tank.

They sat up and stared at the blazing car.

"A complete write-off!" croaked Cuthbert.

Then, slowly at first, but with rapidly gathering momentum, a smile began to spread across *Perkins'* face.

"Well, well, well!" he crowed. "Hoist with your own petard! Serves you jolly well right!"

"If I were you, Perkins," flashed Cuthbert, "I should be careful what I said!"

Perkins openly scoffed.

"I don't *have* to anymore, you old stoat! My dossier

went up in those flames, you old bloodsucker! I'm a free man, now—*free,* I tell you, you old . . ."

The words stopped in his throat, lowered their heads, and muttering, retreated.

For Sir Cuthbert was smiling now. And Sir Cuthbert was slowly shaking his head as he smiled. Sir Cuthbert, smiling, slowly shaking his head, was holding open the top of his coat. With a smile, with a shake, with a swing of the wrist, Sir Cuthbert was showing to Perkins the top edge of the cover of the dossier.

Then he patted it and stood up.

"Let's get back to the rally, shall we?"

A chastened Perkins pointed sullenly to the blazing wreck.

"In that thing?"

Cuthbert was brushing the snow from his clothes.

"My dear Perkins," he said, and his voice was like cold cream, "my dear old clownish retainer, you don't think that with you driving and with so much at stake I did not anticipate either a crackup or a mechanical breakdown?"

He took out another cigar, pierced it with a gold pin, and eyed Perkins with a tinge of disfavor.

"A light, old bean. Or, as they say in that blister Schofield's native land—match me, boy!"

Perkins knew when he was licked. Meekly he took out a box of matches. Sadly, he struck one. Respectfully, he placed it at the end of Cuthbert's cigar.

"So what I did," continued the baronet, when it was nicely drawing and he was able to blow the smoke into Perkins' eyes, "was to arrange for three identical Nifty Nines, with identical numbers, to be planted along the route. A telephone call, and one will be ready by daybreak. . . . But first," he said, turning to the lights of a farmhouse, "let's arrange for transport to a first-class hotel. We can't be very far from Chambéry."

CHAPTER 14

In which chivalry is seen to be not dead.

But Sir Cuthbert was not the only competitor to repair for a good night's rest at Chambéry. Oh no. . . .

Providence, having slipped up so badly over the gasoline notice, must have decided to make amends to the pure in heart and the innocent by arranging for an avalanche of unprecedented volume to block the road from Chambéry to Monte Carlo, even as Ware-Armitage was warming his hands and heart's cockles at the blaze he'd instigated. Indeed, lovers of poetic justice may like to entertain the theory that it was a spark from that blaze, borne on the wind, that settled on the mountain above the road in question and melted the vital inch or two of snow that caused the slight shift that gave rise to the shudder that became the lurch that ended in the avalanche. . . . And why should they not? Perkins, to this day, is convinced of it.

Anyway, whatever the cause, the effect was most certainly this: that the organizers of the rally sent out immediate instructions that the thirty or forty competitors still in the running should stay overnight in Chambéry, while relays of workers plowed a way through the blockage. It was, of course, an arrangement that also gave time for any local gasoline shortage to be made good, thus denying Sir Cuthbert the lead he had so ruthlessly and cunningly schemed for, but he was nothing if not resilient, that one.

In fact, replete with a good meal and the knowledge that as far as dirty tricks were concerned there were plenty more where that last one had come from, it was an almost radiant Cuthbert who stepped from the dining room at Chambéry's second-best hotel that evening. "Almost," we say, because just at that moment there was a power failure, and Cuthbert did not noticeably shed any light around him. Nevertheless, even that little contretemps did nothing to dispel his great good humor, and with no more than a gruff but friendly bark or two, he soon had Perkins at his side, bearing a candle and applying the light to another choice cigar.

"The avalanches must be getting at the power lines, Perkins," he observed. "Either that or the sudden influx of guests has overloaded the hotel wiring. Jolly good job we got here in time to order a good dinner before the grub started running out. By the way, how were the sandwiches I ordered for you?"

Before Perkins could think of an appropriate answer, the lights went on again, revealing a pair of latecomers at the reception desk. They were both well sprinkled with snow, and one was almost buried under the pile of cardboard boxes he was carrying. The other, however, was instantly recognizable.

"That relative of yours," grunted Perkins.

"Yes," murmured Cuthbert, "and the unspeakable Schofield. Well, well. . . ."

With a thoughtful gleam in his eyes he plucked at Perkins' sleeve and drew him toward the stairs and out of sight.

The receptionist was apologizing for the lights, which were still giving the occasional flicker.

"The electricity doesn't normally behave like this, sir. It's the snowstorm farther up. . . . Now, what did you say your names were?"

Chester put down the boxes.

"Chester Schofield the Second and Lady Elizabeth Hardwicke the First."

"Would you sign the book, please. . . . Er . . . I'm afraid there's only one room left. We're rather crowded tonight—" The receptionist nodded toward the groups of disheveled competitors drifting through the lobby. "Is that all right?"

Lesser men would have seized on this chance to do a little sounding out, to drop a sly hint or two. But not Chester. Like a shot he replied:

"No, siree! That is not all right, and I'm surprised at you for even thinking of it. Her ladyship will have the room, and I'll sleep on the Chesterfield in the lobby."

Touched by such chivalry yet loath to cheat nature out of a chance to take her course—for the man was half-French and half-Swiss and a great believer in having it both ways—the receptionist said: "But there's a sofa in the bedroom, sir."

Betty rose to the challenge.

"Then that's what I'll have. You've been doing all the driving, Chester—you have the bed and I'll have the sofa."

The receptionist nodded eagerly.

"No, no," said Chester, and the receptionist's face fell. "You are a girl, so you have the bed and I'll have the sofa."

Brightening again, the receptionist snapped his fingers at a bellhop, and turning to the couple, said: "If you'll both come this way, sir, perhaps you can iron out your sleeping arrangements upstairs."

Now, there were other old friends in that hotel that evening, apart from those we have been observing. There were the two Italians, and the French girls, and Schickel and Schwartz—to say nothing of Dawlish and Barrington. But although this question of sleeping arrangements may have meant little to the receptionist and others like him, to all right-thinking, clean-living men and women it must be causing great concern. In view of this, then, we'd better chaperon the young couple awhile longer.

The bedroom they were shown into was like all the others on the hotel's top floor, with a double bed, a small sofa, a dressing table, a wardrobe, and a luggage rack. None of the guests was to know about this uniformity—yet—but the receptionist did, of course, which makes it permissible for us to mention the matter here. No doubt it was never very far from his thoughts as he showed people to their rooms, even though he might not say it aloud: "This room is like all the others, etc. etc."

Anyway, by now Chester and Betty were beginning to realize just what they'd agreed to and were looking embarrassed and avoiding each other's eyes and pretending the bed wasn't there and so forth—so the receptionist put on a little speed before they started changing their minds and causing him a lot of extra paperwork.

"I assume you wish to be called at seven o'clock, like the other competitors," he said, backing out and pulling the bellhop with him—a lad whose feelings were not at all as delicate.

"I guesh sho," yawned Chester, speeding the boy on his way with a handsome tip, and so confirming in him his worst hopes. "Seven o'clock. . . ."

Betty had already put her boxes on the sofa and Chester's bag on the bed by the time Chester had turned back.

"There!" she said.

Chester blinked.

"Hey! I told you, *you're* to have the bed."

He slipped off his glasses and moved toward the bag.

Then the lights went out.

Chester and Betty stumbled into each other's arms. . . .

Here's what our spotless innocent first said on coming up for air:

"I shouldn't have kissed you, should I?"

Betty smiled, dazed.

"No, I don't think you should—not now, anyway."

Chester gazed dreamily into her eyes.

"Well . . . excuse me . . . I think I'll go wash up."

Then he hurried out, tripping over his bag on the way.

A few seconds later, Sir Cuthbert knocked softly on the door, bearing a glass of warm milk . . . and a potion.

CHAPTER 15

From paradise to purgatory, in less than a thousand words—some of them, toward the end, destined to be uttered in haste.

There was a great deal of to-ing and fro-ing in the corridor outside the room around that time. Not only had Chester gone swinging his sponge bag along it, all unwitting, whistling a Ted Lewis arrangement of "Tiger Rag," and not only had Sir Cuthbert Ware-Armitage come tiptoeing across shortly afterward, as we have already noted—but there were the perambulations and excursions of the other guests to be taken into account.

For instance, no sooner had Betty's door closed behind Cuthbert's back than the two Italians came skulking along. Then, as soon as *they* had rounded the corner, who should come along but Schickel, cursing under his breath and wondering if the pig-dog of a British major had finished with the bathroom yet. Then no sooner had *he* rounded the corner than along came Kit Barrington in regimental pajamas and crested bathrobe, swinging *his* sponge bag; nor had *he* been long out of sight than back came Schickel, still cursing but apparently consoled by the fact that the pig-dog's companion was on a fool's errand also—which was not absolutely correct, for Dawlish himself then appeared, rosy from his tub, indicating that Barrington now had only to wait for Chester. . . .

All in all and by and large, it was rather like Oxford Street or Fifth Avenue when there are only two shopping days left before Christmas, and it was a good five minutes before the coast was sufficiently clear for the reproachful and horrified Perkins to apply eye to keyhole to apprise himself of how his master was faring. But when at last he did so, this, hurriedly, is what he saw:

> Cuthbert
> in front of bed,
> glass of milk in hand.
> Girl staring at him
> with expression
> Perkins
> could feel
> on his own
> f a c e. S i r
> C. placing
> glass milk
> o n t a b l e,
> holding over
> it a folded
> paper spill,
> from which a
> soft white
> powder softly
> pours. Sir C.
> begins softly
> to speak . . .

Whereupon Perkins removed eye and placed ear to keyhole, and this is what he heard:

> It's not as
> if I were asking you to

106

                    do anything difficult. Just
                    persuade young Chester to
                    drink this milk, and
                        all your
                        troubles
                    are over . . .
                        Go on. It
                        won't do
                        him any
                        harm. Just
                        put him to
                        sleep for
                        24 hours.

The girl's reply was lost to Perkins (and to us), for just then he also heard the sound of footsteps and a curious siffilation, and he had to retreat.

The footsteps were Chester's, and the curious siffilation his attempt to whistle "I Want To Be Happy" with right-hand improvisations in the manner of Mr. Earl Hines. For neither tepid water nor the after-odor of the major's manly British carbolic soap had done anything to drive the stars from Chester's eyes. He trod on air, his heart had wings, and he was about to call to mind a list of his favorite things—intending to run through them, boyishly eager, with Betty—when suddenly he stopped.

Dead in his tracks.

Cuthbert was just emerging from Betty's room, and Cuthbert was saying, with admonitory finger at full wag: "Now, do as I tell you, and you'll have no cause to regret it."

Earl Hines departed from the keyboard of Chester's lips and teeth. The young lover's heart's wings developed severe icing trouble, and the only things he could think of now were not at all his favorites really, being like thumbscrews, iron maidens, racks, branding irons, and similar contraptions. But he'd had the presence of mind to step behind a convenient arch, and there he got a grip on himself until Cuthbert had gone back to his own room.

Then he went, tight-lipped, on his way.

Betty was just about to pour the bedeviled milk down the washbasin when he entered.

"And what," asked Chester quietly, "was Sir Cutty doing in here—if that isn't a rude question?"

Betty started. There was no doubt about her guilt, cleverly though she tried to disguise it by putting the glass of milk down on the dressing table, with a casual change of direction.

"Oh, nothing . . . he . . . he came into the wrong room. They're terribly alike, these doors, apparently. And the numbers are so frightfully small."

"Is that so?" said Chester, still quiet, still grim. "And what will you have no cause to regret?"

Betty flushed. *Attack,* ran her family motto, *is the best defense.* She attacked.

"That's none of your business!"

"Oh, yes, it is!" retorted Chester. "I insist on knowing what Sir Cuthbert Ware-Armitage is to you."

"He's my second cousin, if you must know. Grandpa is his uncle."

"Why didn't you tell me this before?"

"Why should I? It's got nothing to do with you."

"Oh no? I have a wager with Sir Armitage—a very, very important one—to him as well as to me. . . . You want to know something? I'm beginning to wonder. . . .

"*What* are you beginning to wonder?" asked Lady Betty, abandoning the bludgeon for the flashing rapier.

Chester brushed it aside—even as his forebears had brushed aside the Indian tomahawks.

"All these delays," he ground on. "All these delays I've been having. Right from the moment I picked you up, little things have been happening to slow us down."

"Such as?"

Lady Betty had rarely looked lovelier than she did now, with blazing eyes and quivering lip. But her jaw was bellicose enough.

Undaunted, Chester—with his wagon train of accusations and suspicions—creaked on.

"*Tea* in Stamford, *cocktails* in Canterbury, *breakfast* in Calais, *shopping* in not-so-gay Paree."

Pocahontas wasn't in it. Betty's eyes contained all the fury of Geronimo and Cochise the Elder combined.

"And you think I deliberately . . . ? *Thank you very much!*"

She picked up her four boxes and fur coat and strode over to the door.

"If it's not delaying you too much," she said with deadly politeness, "would you mind opening the door?"

At which Chester caved in—completely—just like that renegade ancestor who'd suddenly gone native and had started selling guns and firewater to the Sioux.

"There's no need to get all excited, Betty, baby—all I said was—"

But Betty had managed to elbow open the door and was on her way out.

She turned, however—reasonable to the very end.

"And before I go, I'd like to point out that even if I did slow you down once or twice, you're still in Chambéry at the same time as everyone else!"

She stepped outside. Chester made a move to restrain her. She reacted too sharply and dropped her boxes. It was the last straw.

With tears springing from her eyes, she swore loud and (for her) violently.

"Oh, blast! Oh, blazes! Oh, bee-ell-ai-ess-tee!"

Chester tried to help, but she pushed him away.

He retired to his room.

Almost beside himself with grief and distraction, he tottered blindly to the dressing table.

He saw but did not see the glass of milk.

Automatically he picked it up.

Without thinking, he lifted it to his lips.

Then the thought of the sudden swoop from highest bliss struck him viciously, right below the belt, and he too cursed violently (for him). "Oh bee-ell-ai-ess-tee!" he swore.

And he put down the glass, took off his jacket, loosened his tie, and flopped down miserably upon the bed.

The milk—it should be noted—was left untasted.

As yet. . . .

Throughout that night there was a great deal of confusion in the corridors. It arose from the fact that the rooms were not plainly numbered. Most of the guests were using as markers the sight of their own shoes, placed outside the doors for cleaning. This seemed a sensible idea—until Sir Cuthbert switched the shoes around—cackling evilly. Then, with the repeated failure of the lights making matters worse, there was such a screaming and a cursing and a bellowing and a shrinking and a chasing and a threatening and a protesting that it looked as if Cuthbert's scheme (to rob his rivals of a good night's rest) would be one hundred per cent successful.

Imagine Chester's relief when, a few hours later, he found Betty down in the lobby, lying peacefully asleep on the Chesterfield in front of a log fire.

Gently he nudged her shoulder.

"Betty?"

There was no reply.

He tried again.

"Are you asleep?"

She blinked, then turned over.

"Yes. And I don't want to speak to you. . . . I'm terribly sleepy."

"Yeah, well, I'm sleepy too. But I can't go to sleep until I've said I'm sorry."

No reply.

"I mean, I guess I jumped to the most horrible conclusions about you. Gee whizz, I ought to have my head examined. A wonderful girl like you couldn't possibly have . . . Well, what I mean . . . without your help I'd never even have gotten as far as *this.*"

Such music to a woman's ears didn't go unnoticed.

Betty looked up sympathetically.

"The fact of the matter is," continued Chester, much encouraged, "I'm so sleepy I don't know what to do except say I'm sorry."

Betty sat up sharply at this, remembering the milk.

"You didn't drink—"

"No, no—I haven't been drinking."

"Oh, thank goodness!" gasped Betty, relaxing.

She sank back on the sofa.

"I mean, I can't stand a man who drinks," she said, noticing his puzzled expression.

"I've given it up," said Chester, relaxing in turn. "I threw the flask away . . . you saw me. And I only had orange juice for cocktails in Canterbury."

She smiled and patted the sofa beside her.

"I forgive you."

Chester sat down.

"Thank you. . . ." He looked around. "Do you think

it would be O.K. if I kinda huddled down beside you for a moment?"

She didn't reply, but then neither did she resist as he wriggled down next to her, under the fur coat.

"I really am sorry, and I do love you." He closed his eyes. "Did I tell you that before?"

"No, you didn't," said Betty eagerly. "Tell me it again, do!"

But Chester was too sleepy. All she got in answer was a long, deep, slow snore.

And he'd not even drunk the milk by then. . . .

CHAPTER 16

A confession—coming, as most of them do, too late in the day to be of much practical value to the victim of the originating misdemeanor.

"Chester! Chester!"

The owner of that name blinked, licked his lips. In his dream he'd just been about to reply to a deputation that had called upon him and his beautiful British lady-wife with the request that he take over the Presidency of the United States of America forthwith.

"Later," he mumbled, "busy righ' now. . . ."

"Chester!"

He blinked again. The morning sunlight hurt his eyes, but he braved it sufficiently to note that he was lying on the floor of some European hotel lobby and that the person yelling at him was his lady-wife-elect herself, sitting bolt upright on a Chesterfield.

"What is it? What goes on? I told you I cut out the drinking. . . ."

"Chester! They're all going!"

"Who's all going?"

"The rally. The other competitors. Look!"

He staggered to his feet and gaped out of the window. Already some of the cars were driving away, making good time up the hill, through which a track had been cut with snow plows. Others were handing in their logbooks

113

at a small hut set up as a temporary checkpoint and having them stamped by an official.

"Oh, yeah!" yawned Chester. "The rally. . . ."

"Well, don't just stand there!" urged Betty. "I'll get dressed as quickly as I can behind this screen."

"Yeah. Dressed," grunted Chester.

Then suddenly coming to life, he rushed to the stairs and climbed them three at a time.

As soon as she was dressed, Betty followed to see if she could help him pack. But alas for her—and alas even more for him—she was just in time to see him, bag and coat in hand, pick up the glass of milk, mutter, "Breakfast, breakfast, no time, this'll do"—and gulp it down.

"NO!!" she screamed.

Too late.

"What's the matter?" asked Chester, blinking around, mild as milk (undoctored) himself.

"That milk! Oh, gosh! It—it was drugged."

Chester's face dropped three or four notches.

"What?!"

Betty groaned.

"That's why Cuthbert was here last night. He was trying to force me to make you drink it."

"*Force* you? How could he do that?"

Betty's lip was quivering—but this time with chagrin and despair.

"He—he knows something terrible about Grandpa. Something that could get him unfrocked. He said if I didn't want this to happen I would have to do what he wanted. . . . I mean, you see now how I was placed. It would be terrible for Grandpa, being a bishop."

"It isn't exactly chopped chicken liver for me," grunted Chester.

He flopped down upon the bed.

Man—even optimistic young American man—can take just so much.

"Well, I guess that's it," he sighed. "I guess I lose everything."

She grabbed his arm. Beautiful British lady-wives-elect of potential candidates for the American Presidency are made of pretty tough stuff.

"Oh, no, you won't!" she said. "Do you feel sleepy yet?"

Chester sat up and took a peek at himself in the mirror.

"Well, no . . . as a matter of fact, I feel quite good."

"Come on, then. You never know. It may not work with you. And anyway—I'll keep you awake."

Chester got to his feet.

"You will? How?"

"I'll sing to you, throw water over you, anything—but you must keep going. . . . So come along . . . quickly. . . ."

Chester nodded.

"O.K. . . . quickly. . . . We've got to keep going! We've got to keep going!"

But, as students of such diversions as *Chiller Theater* and *Journey into the Unknown* will have realized, there was a disturbing zombielike automaton note about his repetitive mumblings already.

"May not work on *him*" indeed!

CHAPTER 17

How smoke got into Sir Cuthbert's eyes and the
Wheel of Fortune got into Major Dawlish's way.

Meanwhile, although he wasn't enjoying the flying start
he'd anticipated, the author of this foul deed was faring
pretty nicely, thank you. Waiting to greet him and Perkins as they strode out into the parking lot that morning
was the brand-new Nifty Nine Sir Cuthbert had spoken of
the night before—gleaming under its light sprinkling of
snow and identical in every respect with the one that had
been burned.

"There you are, Perkins. A dead ringer."

Perkins lowered the bags he'd been staggering under
and gaped.

"You amaze me!"

What he meant was the bare-faced cheek of his master.
Cuthbert took it to mean his strategic brilliance.

"You've got to get up early in the morning to catch a
Ware-Armitage!" he purred.

Perkins climbed onto the running board to put the baggage on the roof rack just as Cuthbert was opening the
driver's door, eager to try out the new car. This sent Perkins sprawling over the hood and a suitcase banging into
the bodywork.

"Be careful, blast you!" snarled Cuthbert. "This is a
brand-new . . ."

116

He trailed off, his eye caught by a little cameo taking place on the other side of the lot.

Had this been anywhere else, Cuthbert would have put it down to an advance publicity stunt on behalf of a three-ring circus. But although the object being fitted to the car there—with much crashing and banging and flailing of hammers and wrenches—had all the appearance of a cowcatcher filched from the Canadian Pacific Railroad Company, the clowns at work on it were recognizable as fellow competitors and Englishmen.

"All right, Barrington, that'll do," commanded the major after a few more belts with the wrench. He picked up an oil can and proceeded to pour oil into the contraption. "Now, then," he said, straightening up and putting out a hand on the blind side with all the delicate crispness of a brain surgeon. "Blowtorch. . . . Thank you. . . . Stand back!"

He aimed the torch at the mechanized monstrosity. There was a woosh of flame. He was knocked off his feet. But there was a bright gleam in his eyes as he stood up and gazed at the snow that was now rapidly melting in front of the Lea Francis.

"By Jove, Barrington, it's working!" he barked. "If the Dawlish Snow-Melter doesn't see us through to Monte, then my name's Rudolph Valentino!"

Barrington beamed.

"This must be a proud moment for you, sir!"

"It is, Barrington, it is. I think I can truthfully say I'm on my way to my first million."

"Oh, whizz-whizz, sir! How absolutely rip-rip-ripping!"

Sir Cuthbert watched with immense interest as they climbed into the Lea Francis and drove off, leaving a trail of black smoke.

"That cowcatcher thing's melting the snow, sir," said Perkins. "Why don't we follow it?"

Cuthbert bent on him an approving leer.

"A good idea! . . . You know, Perkins, some of my genius seems to be rubbing off on to you at last."

Then he too drove off.

Some three-quarters of an hour later, Sir Cuthbert wasn't at all sure about this transference of genius. For although the Dawlish Snow-Melter was still doing its stuff, the smoke was abominable, increasing in volume and density the higher they climbed. Furthermore, the cold was getting so intense up there that the melted snow was beginning to freeze again by the time the Nifty Nine reached it, and Cuthbert was having a job to keep the car from slithering off the road.

"What a silly idea that was of yours!" he choked. "They're putting up a smoke screen too."

"Must be naval men, sir," said Perkins brightly.

Cuthbert glared at him, then noticed a side turning a little way ahead.

"This must be the high road," he said. "We'll take it. They can have the low road to their beastly selves."

"And we'll be in Scotland afore them!" sang Perkins.

"One more joke like that," snarled Cuthbert, turning off, "and Mrs. Perkins will certainly see the dossier!"

But it was slippery up there too, and as they skidded around a bend shortly afterward, the spare wheel was jerked off, and down, down, down . . .

. . . it bounced, right in front of the Lea Francis on the lower road.

Dawlish took avoiding action but took it too late. Into a boulder skidded the car, and into a compact concertinaed mass of pig iron went the Snow-Melter, slowly oozing black oil.

They got out and stared at it in dismay.

"Oh, shame, shame, sir!" cried Kit. "It's broken!"

Dawlish shook his head.

"Rotten civilian workmanship!" he murmured. "Should have had it made by the army."

He bent to examine it.

"Bang goes your first million, eh, sir?" said Kit, wanting to express his sympathy. (Which brings out yet another difference between his and Perkins' doormatship—for, as we have seen, the latter would have displayed a marked tendency to crow under similar circumstances.)

"All part of the game, Barrington," sighed Dawlish, rising. "Rip it off. We may have lost the Melter, but we haven't lost the Monte."

"Oh, well said, sir!" cried Kit. "And so elegantly, too. . . . Are we going to change to the Dawlish Super Snow Tractor now, sir?"

"Exactly. A good soldier always has something in reserve."*

"That's what I always say, sir!"

Then they hurried around to the back of the car and started hauling off a length of caterpillar tread from the Dawlish Hold-All—little knowing that what was spelling delay for them was to be a decisive factor in saving the life of another competitor not long afterward.

---

*We would recommend to senior students the following topic for essays and dissertations: "The Cuthbert-Perkins and Dawlish-Barrington Syndromes: A Comparison and Contrasting of the Two Relationships." After all, what was this last remark of Dawlish's but a significant variant of Sir Cuthert's axiom: "A Ware-Armitage always has a few more cards up his sleeve"?

CHAPTER 18

*Another Wheel, another Fortune, culminating in
Lady Betty's dicing with Death.*

Schickel and Schwartz—whose night had been rather
more hectic than most of the others'—were running late,
even later than Betty and Chester. In spite of this, a
happy humming was issuing from Willi's lips as he drove
the Mercedes along a road made more treacherous by the
ravages of the Dawlish Snow-Melter and the ruts of the
other competitors. He was, after all, a driver first and a
criminal afterward—not long afterward, to be sure, but
afterward nonetheless—and he was beginning to regard
the increasing difficulties as a challenge. Indeed, he was
beginning to step up the speed way above what seemed
safe from more than one standpoint.

Otto voiced it thus: "Are we not going too fast, Willi?
His Excellency is definitely saying we must finish in twenty-sixth position."

Schickel spat.

"Who is caring what his Excellency is saying?" he

jeered. "We are Germans, and there is only one place for
a German, and that is first."

"*Ja. . . . Ja*, Willi. But we are not ordinary Germans,
and his Excell— Ayeee!"

A loud report and a sudden violent bucking of the

Mercedes had interrupted him. Schickel struggled with the wheel. The car slithered to a stop.

"Ein blowout," grunted Willi.

Sure enough, the nearside-front tire was torn to shreds.

"Jack her up," ordered Schickel, going around the back to get one of the spares.

The sight of them stacked there plucked at his heartstrings. He glanced around to make sure that Otto was busily occupied. Then he pulled off the top two spares and compared the weights. His eyes brightened as he noted that one was distinctly heavier. Rapidly he cut the tape binding. He felt around inside. He started. Tears of joy sprang sparkling from his eyes. Even Otto's sudden approach couldn't dampen the joy that Willi felt then.

"Is it the one with the stuff?" gasped Otto.

"It is the one with the stuff," said Willi, peering inside and blinking, dazzled by what he saw. "And the stuff is chewellss. All taped to the inside. Big fat glittering chewellss, Otto!"

Otto gaped down in awe. He lowered his voice.

"If his Excellency is taking all this trouble to get them to Monte Carlo, they must be worth many many rubles, Willi."

"Many rubles, Otto," whispered Willi. His eyes narrowed. "So why don't we keep them for ourselves?"

Otto shivered. His eyes flitted from side to side.

"Ach, nein, nein, Willi! His Excellency is too powerful. He is having eyes everywhere."

"Everywhere, Otto?"

Willi gazed around at the desolate landscape.

"Even *here?"* Willi chuckled. "Otto! Otto! You are a stupid fellow to believe that. Why don't we make for Switzerland—now—immediately? They would never find us there."

"But they would trace the car."

"So we go by foot," said Schickel—and without further ado he slung the spare tire over his shoulder and chest like a bandolier and stalked off, followed by the complaining Otto.

But Willi had not gone farther than a dozen paces when the shots rang out. Two of them.

The men jumped clean out of their footprints.

"Vass ist dass?" breathed Schickel, crouching close to the snow.

"See!" hissed Schwartz.

He pointed to a bush about half a mile away.

Two puffs of smoke were slowly drifting above it.

Then Otto started again and pointed to his left.

"Look!"

There was a flashing, as of semaphore signals, from a mountainside.

"Come!" gasped Schickel, lumbering back to the Mercedes.

"But where, Willi?"

"To Monte Carlo, you *dumkopf!* Twenty-sixth position."

He flung the tire into the back seat and hurriedly got another from the pile. There was a third shot. As Otto feverishly worked to replace the punctured tire, Willi leaped up and down, hands waving in the air.

"Kamarad! Your Excellency! Don't shoot! We only make *der* little joke! Now, see, we are changing the tire!"

Some twenty seconds later the repair had been made and the Mercedes was shooting off to Monte Carlo with all the dispatch of a rocket.

"Well, well," murmured the Alpine hunter who had been watching all this from a distance with some perplexity. "These rally drivers! Crazy!"

And, picking up the brace of rabbits he had just shot, he trudged off to where he'd left his small son amusing himself with a mirror.

The zooming past of the Mercedes a mile or two farther along helped Betty to make up her mind. The Triple S had been weaving from side to side most alarmingly, and it was a wonder the German car hadn't gone smack into them.

"You've got to stop for a moment, Chester," she pleaded. "I'll walk you up and down the road in the cold air."

Chester was shaking his head in an effort to clear it.

"I can't stop. I've got to beat Sir Armitage."

Even so, the car slowed down and came to a jerky stop.

". . . Zzzrrr Rrrrumtage . . ." repeated Chester.

Betty looked at him desperately. Then, taking his chin between the finger and thumb of her left hand, she gave his face three or four hearty slaps with her right.

"Oh, Chester! Are you all right? Do wake up!" (Slap!) "Please!" (Slap!) "I love you!" (Splatz!) "I love you, Chester!"

She underlined this last remark by grabbing his hair and whacking his head against the steering wheel—but that was no good either.

"If only I could drive!" she moaned, raising her lovely eyes heavenward. Then she frowned, pouting a little. "Still, why not? It can't be all that difficult. I mean, so many people *do* drive these days—even Grandpa. And if he can, I jolly well can!"

Was the spirit of Britannia abroad among the mountaintops that day? If so she must surely have sent a triumphant yodel or two echoing around the valleys, as this

E. W. Hildick

brave lass, this daughter of Albion, hauled Chester across
into the passenger seat and took over the wheel herself.

Betty pressed the accelerator.

The car revved up.

But it didn't move.

"Oh, dear, what have I forgotten?" she murmured.

She thought hard.

"Ah, yes! The joystick."

She got hold of the gearshift, and with a noise like the
climax of an Art Blakey solo, slammed it home. The car
jerked forward.

"Ooh!" squealed the girl. "I must let the brake out another notch, mustn't I?"

She let it out completely, and the car shot forward.

"Ooh!" she squealed again. "It does make a difference!"

Britannia, it seemed, was looking after her own that afternoon.

It didn't take Betty long to get the feel of the thing.
And it took not a second longer for her to feel exceed-
ingly pleased with herself. Some might say smug. The
perceptive few might even qualify it further by saying
dangerously smug.

"Oh, Chester!" she murmured. "I do wish you could
see me. I'm driving your Six Sylinder Special incorporating overhead carbs and double cam."

"Zzzzrrr . . . Rhummitage . . ." replied the uncon-
scious Chester.

Betty concentrated on the road ahead. It was shifting
about from side to side in a manner not entirely conform-
ing to its natural twists and bends, and it was rising with-
al. But since the car was in low gear, no serious prob-
lem was being presented at that stage. The going was dis-

tinctly bumpy, too, but what mattered that? Betty even found the heart to sing a line or two about the rolling English drunkards building rolling English roads, and another few lines on the subject of Britannia ruling the waves, and she was just about to launch herself into the refrain of that catchy little ditty about ducks being a-dabbling up tails all, when the Triple S reached the top and went over the crest and uptailed herself. Or so it seemed as they began to plunge down what looked like a one-in-one gradient at the other side.

"Chester!" screamed Betty. "Wake up! Wake up!"

"Zzzzrrrumtage . . ." was the only reply she was vouchsafed.

Skidding, bumping, lurching, and increasing speed all the time, the Triple S went hurtling down the hill. . . .

It was a beautiful route really. Picturesque boulders loomed here, towering firs there, but it took the girl all her time to evade them, leaving none to contemplate them or seek to divine the secret of their somber beauty.

Even the gigantic waterfall to the left—the yellow-white torrent dropping down from a higher point through slabs of ice and jagged rock for hundreds of rugged feet, down into a ravine and out of sight from the road—even that would not have attracted her gaze for longer than a thousandth of a second, had not the Triple S just then gone skidding completely out of control over the side of the road and straight toward this masterpiece of nature.

CHAPTER 19

A chapter proving that true melodrama is not dead, beginning with an Act of Villainy the like of which has never been seen before, and proceeding to a Breathtaking Acrobatic Performance without a safety net.

The Nifty Nine had still been on the high road when Betty had woven her hectic way along the lower, so that it came as a double shock to Perkins, now at the wheel and back on the lower road himself, to see the Triple S again, and in such a predicament.

Scarcely able to believe it, he pulled up at the side of the road.

The fur-lined mound in the back seat rose up indignantly.

"What's the matter, Perkins?" it demanded. "Can't you wait?"

"Look!" said Perkins, pointing across the snow up toward the gigantic half-frozen cascade.

"We are not here to admire the scenery, you oaf! Get—"

Then Sir Cuthbert suddenly saw what all the fuss was about.

They were quite a bit lower down the hill than the spot where the Triple S had taken off, so that the sight was all the more spectacular—the sight, that is, not so much of the waterfall as of the rocky promontory in front of it, and of the car that was teetering on its edge, one half al-

126

ready swaying over the ravine in the spray from the fall. There was at least another hundred feet to go beneath this spot—and go is precisely what the Triple S looked like doing, given an extra puff of wind or another ounce or two of spray on its hood.

The slow grin spread across Cuthbert's face even as he stared.

"I say," he murmured, "good work, Betty, old girl! Schofield'll never get out of that!" He turned to his companion. "Shake hands with the winner, Perkins!"

With a little shudder, Perkins ignored the outstretched hand and got out of the car.

"You've gone too far this time," he said. "They're still inside it, I think."

He set off toward the swaying car.

Cuthbert caught him by the sleeve.

"Where d'you think you're going?"

"Up there to help them, of course."

"What?" sneered Cuthbert. "Without your galoshes?"

"It's the only decent thing to do."

Sir Cuthbert snorted.

"Oh, cut out all that Scott of the Antarctic stuff, or I'll get out myself and give the blasted thing a push!"

Perkins' face wrinkled up in disgust.

"You wouldn't!" Then his eyes widened and he gulped. "You would, at that!" he croaked.

"Of course I would!" snapped Cuthbert, who'd never had time for ditherers. "Now, get in and shut up!"

Dragging his feet, sighing heavily, but knowing, as ever, when he'd met his match, Perkins did as he was told.

Fortunately Betty had not witnessed this scene, otherwise she might have lost heart completely. As it was, she was almost too scared to breathe.

"Chester!" she whispered.

And the car swayed a whisper more strongly.

"Chester! Wake up!"

The swaying became a gentle rocking.

"Please!"

She patted him sharply on the cheek, and the rocking became less gentle.

But it did the trick.

Chester blinked.

Betty was glad but wished he wouldn't flutter his eyelashes so strongly.

"Trouble?" murmured Chester drowsily.

To have said, "Trouble indeed!" or, "Yes, Big Trouble!" was more than she dared venture. Instead she merely pointed over the side.

Chester sat up, and the rocking was augmented by a slight rolling. He took off his glasses, conscious of her nearness, and Betty thought she would faint.

"It can't be as bad as that, honey," he said, and she gave thanks to heaven for having ordained that he be such a soft-spoken young man in the natural way of things. "Relax! I'll take a look."

And there wasn't a thing she could do about it save bend her body in an equal and opposite direction to counteract the effects of Chester's movement.

Or *almost* equal. And not *quite* opposite.

For Chester, without his glasses, had blithely opened the door, stepped out, and vanished.

Betty shrieked, and maybe that prolonged their lives, doing something to compensate for the lurch the car gave when Chester grabbed the running board, just in time. . . .

He looked down.

His eyes nearly popped out of his head—a movement, slight though it was, that nearly tipped the balance.

The hundred-foot drop below looked more like half a mile.

But he'd had the benefits of a technological training.

"Betty," he murmured, rather like a ventriloquist, chary of too much tongue or lip movement, "cly carely inqua ack eat." Which she, clever girl that she was, interpreted correctly as: "Climb carefully into the back seat."

But she wasn't so clever as to realize what Chester was getting at. *She'd* never been taught all that stuff about fulcrums and moments about a point. Instead, she took a peek over the side—and nearly passed out again. The swaying became a swinging.

"Betty, do as I *ay, ease!*"

"I—I can't! I'm too scared!"

"Honey, please!" said Chester, risking the fully mobile mouth, the better to make his point. "Because if you don't, we're both going down there."

"All—all right, then. . . ."

Carefully, slowly, trembling, she started to inch her way over into the back seat.

The car's forward dip began to correct itself as she did so. Chester then tried to pull himself up on the running board.

He was aiming at turning himself over and up, like a trapeze artist, and so gaining a foothold. He nearly did it, too, but slipped, fell upside-down, and ended the movement clinging like a bat to the underparts of the by now violently bucking car.

"You'll have to get help!" he called up hoarsely.

"How can I?" she wailed back. "I don't know anyone here."

But even as she spoke, a chugging sound made her turn.

Her eyes widened.
A glimmer of hope appeared in them.
"Just a minute. . . ." she said.

Was this a mirage? Or could help really be on the way?

CHAPTER 20

Proving once and for all that the resemblance between the Cuthbert-Perkins and Dawlish-Barrington partnerships is purely superficial, with our profound apologies to the latter for ever having thought otherwise.

It was not a mirage.

It was almost as weird—being the Lea Francis toiling down the hill equipped with its caterpillar tracks. But damsels in distress have no time to be fussing over the appearance of their potential rescuers' modes of transport, as the old Chinese saying, freely translated, has it. On the contrary, such a damsel's first duty is to attract the attention of such a potential rescuer, and this the Lady Betty Hardwicke right lustily did.

Kit it was who first heard her.

He glanced across the snowy waste—then stared.

"I say, sir, don't think I'm being facetious—but I really do think that lady over there is in difficulties."

Major Dawlish turned to see where he was pointing—then stared himself.

"By Jove, you're right, Kit!" he said, suddenly feeling all medieval and Arthurian. " 'Tis a damsel in distress," he quod, remembering that this was the way all rescuing knights carried on. "Gramercy and godsookers!"

"Quickly! Oh, please, help!"

131

"And English too, forsooth!"

Which settlinge it, this knight si vertuous yclept D'Owlish let in the clutche and sped across the icy wasters first to gain the catyrpelers' purchase, this being strongermost at the hinder end of his trustie steed, and avaunt, eftsoons like the bells of boggartry, cursed be our soules if he did not nearly collyde with the steed of the knight of the Triple Esse, which would in truth have put an end to our tayle erewith. Full certain it is that this nere-miss knocked all the courtly codswallop clean out of D'Owlish's head, and he became straight Major Dawlish again as he jumped out to take a better look at the situation.

"Hang on, sir," Barrington was calling to Chester, having noticed the direction of Betty's horrified gaze. "Nothing to worry about. The army's here."

Had Custer himself appeared, Chester couldn't have felt more relieved. Even so, he dared do no more than utter an appreciative glug.

Then Dawlish swung crisply into his stride and took charge.

"Barrington, I should go down the north face if I were you and make contact with him from there. It's a lot easier. I'll take care of the lady." Keeping a firm grip on the car, he helped her out gingerly. "There, there, madam. Nothing to worry about. You're in excellent hands."

Kit slid slowly down past the car until he was level with Chester. Then, stretching out one of his excellent hands, he caught hold of Chester's belt. Next he took hold of the stranded hero with his other excellent hand and worked his way down Chester's body until he was sitting astride the other's impeccable right foot.

"Are you all right, sir?" he asked anxiously.

Chester, sweating under the extra burden, managed a weak, "Oh, sure! I'm fine!"

Having established contact with the party to be rescued, Barrington took the second essential step.

"May I introduce myself? My name is Kit Barrington, Sixteenth Lancers."

He held his unimpeachable right hand upward, and Chester—not to be outdone in politeness by an Englishman—let go of the running board with his own absolutely splendid right hand, and they exchanged greetings as two civilized human beings should.

"Chester Schofield the Second," he even managed to gasp. "Thirteen Rivington Street."

The car lurched again. He hastily regained his grip on the running board.

"Come along, Barrington! Don't dawdle!"

Major Dawlish had allowed a testy note to edge into his voice. After all, it was no joke being stuck up there, with all the responsibility of command on one's shoulders, fanning a fainting girl with one's cap and hanging on to the rear end of a swaying car with one's free hand.

The car gave an extra lurch in response. Betty almost swooned again. Then, to her great relief, Barrington and Chester came scrambling over the snowy edge of the drop.

Chester had just enough time to thank Kit before dropping off to sleep in Betty's arms.

As Dawlish and Barrington made fast the Dawlish Patent Tow Rope to the rear of the Triple S, Betty led Chester, snoring by now but just capable of tottering under her guidance, to less slippery ground.

"Hallo!" called a female voice. "Anyone hurt? Do you need help?"

It was one of the French girls. They were hurrying across the snow from their Peugeot.

133

"No," said Betty. "But Chester does. He's been doped. He can't keep awake."

She took a handful of snow and rubbed it over Chester's face.

The sleeper opened his eyes, squinting as he focused the girls.

"I feel swell. . . . I really do!"

The leader of the French girls snorted learnedly.

"Swell? . . . I am a doctor. I do not think you are so well."

She took Chester's pulse and frowned.

"Do you really want to continue?"

"I've got to!" groaned Chester.

"Come with me, then," said Marie-Claude.

She led them down to her car.

After rummaging in a very medical-looking case, she brought out a bottle of pills. She knocked a couple into her hand and passed them to Chester.

"These are something new, and normally I would not prescribe them. They will clear your head and keep you going for twenty-four hours . . . after that, well, there'll be a reaction that will make the drug you have already taken seem like aspirin. You will sleep and sleep and sleep. . . ."

Chester didn't hesitate. Unless there were any unforeseen delays, twenty-four hours would be just enough to see him through to the end of the rally.

"Thanks a lot, doc!" he said, and gulped down the pills.

But before anyone starts ordering the champagne, just remember the bit about unforeseen delays—a bit which by rights and according to the way of this world of ours should have been presented in the smallest possible print.

CHAPTER 21

Of optimism in its various forms, ranging from pure blind wishful-thinking optimism to the optimism that is underpinned with certain practical precautions.

The lobby of the Hotel de Paris in Monte Carlo was thronged that evening. Rally drivers, officials, and journalists drifted around chatting animatedly. For this, if not precisely It, was the Eve of It, and even the weariest of competitors had found new strength and vigor in the general excitement.

The main topic of conversation was naturally the decision about the race-off the following morning. As Monsieur Dupont, the chief organizer, had announced earlier in the day, the rally that year had been too badly beset with difficulties, confusions, irregularities, and accidents for the usual points system to be strictly adhered to. Therefore the thirty or so competitors who had eventually made it to Monte Carlo, or were on the point of so doing, and who were virtually neck and neck as far as their totals were concerned, were to have a time trial around the Grande Corniche. This, it was generally agreed, would settle the whole thing, producing a clear-cut winner, and many were the bets that were being laid or opinions ventured as to who this was likely to be.

Some felt it was bound to go to the Mercedes, with

135

such an experienced driver as Horst Muller at the wheel. Others were inclined to fancy the Lea Francis, with its battery of gadgets and a rumored Rocket Booster still under (red, white, and blue) wraps. Others still declined to write off the Triple S, with its Anglo-American crew, in spite of the fact that it had not yet arrived in Monte Carlo, and of reports of a strange sickness that seemed to have overtaken the American half of the team. The fly, the knowing, the cold-eyed professional punters in the throng smiled indulgently at all this chat—calculating that if the Nifty Nine had reached this stage without disqualification, nothing on earth could deprive Cuthbert Ware-Armitage of the trophy—short of a full-scale investigation by the combined forces of the Sûreté and Scotland Yard, for which there was hardly time now. On the other hand, the soft, the sentimental, and the unashamedly romantic were plumping for the Lancia. After all, had not the two Italians openly declared that they were in there now to win not only for themselves, their country, and their future careers as gentlemen drivers of independent means, beautiful wives, and large families, but also for the French girls, who had so generously written themselves out of the running earlier that day.

And this was the second of the main topics of conversation. It seemed that after Marie-Claude and her friends had extended a helping hand to Chester, they had gone on to surpass themselves in Good Samaritanship when they'd encountered a rather nasty accident farther along the route and had volunteered to remain with the injured. Angelo and Marcello, who had also been on the scene, had gallantly offered to stay themselves instead, but when the girls pointed out that their long training as doctors rather outweighed in medical usefulness the three-day course in First Aid given to the policemen of Rome, the men saw the sense of this. Nevertheless, Angelo was moved to announce that: "If we win, we will tell everyone that you would have beaten us."

Touching, very, agreed the cold-eyed punters. But dumb, stupid, and out of the question.

Now there was also a third important topic being discussed in the hotel lobby that evening—but *in camera*, in frantic whispers, behind a thick hedge of potted palms, by Herren Willi Schickel and Otto Schwartz—and it was this:

The count and Waleska had been arrested on the steps of the casino that very afternoon. There was no doubt about it whatsoever, for the incident had occurred at the very moment of the Mercedes' arrival, and the four men had actually come face to face. Indeed, for a brief moment it had looked as if the count had been about to put the finger on Willi and Otto, too. He had paused, he had stared, he had opened his mouth. But then he had lifted his manacled hands to his face, removed his eyeglass, polished it, put it back, and gone on to the police car without a word.

Willi and Otto were still debating this.

"I tell you it was a message, Willi. He meant us to know something by that action."

"*Ja,* but what message? Await further instructions? Flee? Send the chewelss to *mein* lawyers? What?"

"Whatever it was, Willi, I say let's go. Now. Before we too are arrested."

Schickel shook his head. There was a glint in his eyes. His mind was made up.

"The count will not betray us to the police, whatever his future plans for us might be. So why *not* stay another few hours? Why not take the chewelss *and* the trophy? Forget *der* twenty-sixth position. I am going to win that speed test. Then even if, as the calf said in the slaughter-house, the worse comes to *der wurst,* I shall go back to *mein* prison a happy wanderer."

And that settled that. . . .

Not far from the scene of this momentous secret conference, Sir Cuthbert was moving through the crowd with a cigar in his mouth and his ears alert for the offer of juicy odds on the Nifty Nine. Then a sudden thought struck him with all the impact of a sharp-pointed boot in the lower gut.

He winced and looked around hurriedly until he spotted Perkins.

He signaled.

Perkins came.

"Where the dickens have you been?" demanded Cuthbert.

"I was just having a bath, sir."

"Well, you might have washed the car first. . . . But never mind that now. There's a rather more important job to be done."

And he drew Perkins out through the swing doors and into the night.

"But I don't see—"

"Of course you don't, Perkins. I nearly overlooked it myself. Listen . . . the only thing that could possibly count heavily against us is the spare tire we lost."

They were now in the parking lot, where the Nifty Nine stood out among the others, comparatively dirt-free and certainly dentless.

"Oh, bad luck, sir!" said Perkins, audibly cheered.

"Luck, Perkins, is not going to enter into it. We're going to replace that tire."

"But where d'you think you're going to get one at this time of the night?"

"I'm not getting one," said Cuthbert. *"You* are."

"Me?"

Cuthbert jabbed his cigar in the direction of the nearby Mercedes.

"That blighter's got more than he needs. They'll never notice if one is missing."

"But—but that's *stealing*, sir!"

"Rubbish! Don't be so technical. Get on with it."

Perkins crept unwillingly to the back of the Mercedes. With reluctant fingers, wondering where all this would end, he began to unstrap the belt that held the tires in place. But before he could get very far with it, another car entered the parking lot, and its headlights flashed across him. He froze, then jumped into the shadows at the side, telling himself that *here* apparently was where all this would end.

The beam lingered. Crouching, he opened the door of the Mercedes and slipped into the back seat. Fear gripped his bowels, even as he felt something else gripping him slightly lower down. But slowly, to his vast relief, the beam swung away, leaving him in darkness.

He started to get out, then found he was stuck.

He opened his mouth to scream—for it was as if a monster with toothless but powerful gums had clamped its jaws on his backside. Then he realized it was nothing more sinister than yet another spare tire.

Perkins was a firm believer in a bird in the hand being worth two in the bush, and even though that was not his hand and this was no bird, he settled for the tire in question—once, after some tricky contortions and a helping hand from Cuthbert, he'd managed to get himself unstuck.

The helping hand was still holding the fiercely glowing cigar—but that's irrelevant here.

The spare tire thus selected was still holding the secretly sparkling jewels—and that is not irrelevant.

Now, the headlights that had so rudely interrupted Perkins' unwilling act of larceny had, in fact, belonged to the Triple S. And, far from wishing to pry into Perkins' personal business, Chester and Betty had been much too anxious to make sure of their rooms even to notice him.

"Not that I'm tired at all right now," said Chester as they hurried in. "In fact, I'd like to go dancing or something! I guess it's those pills. I wonder what was in them? I feel like a million dollars."

"*I* feel like tuppence ha'penny," said Betty dejectedly, once they were in the privacy of her room.

Chester turned to her, taking her arm.

"How's this? Did I do something wrong?"

She shook her head, slowly, sadly.

"No. *I* did. . . ." She looked up at him. "I have to tell you, Chester. When you first picked me up on the Yorkshire moors—it wasn't by chance."

"Sir Cutty sent you there?"

Betty nodded.

"I was to do a terrible thing. . . . I was supposed to lure you back to Bardsley Manor—"

"—and spend the rest of the day having tea with your grandfather. I know. But I don't care."

"You—you don't care? Not even if I told you I had to borrow money from Ware-Armitage in Paris? . . . You *can't* like me."

"I do care, and I do like you," declared Chester roundly then. "So much that I'm going to go out on that circuit tomorrow and grind Sir Cutty's nose into the ground for blackmailing you and your grandpa! And then I'm going to come right back here, take out this handkerchief, put it on the floor, kneel on it, and say . . ." He smiled at the expression on her face. "That drug the lady gave me's gone to my head, I guess."

It has, Chester, it has! But only for about twenty-four

hours, remember. And isn't the race-off scheduled for a time in the late morning that in your case could mean cutting things rather fine?

We shall soon see, anyway. . . . .

CHAPTER 22

*The race-off, with notes on the principal runners,
their form and failings.*

Next day, as the cars lined up for the start of the time
trial, in the square opposite the casino terrace, a hush fell
over the huge crowd gathered there. It was as if each
man, woman, and child could feel what was at stake for
each of the twenty-eight drivers involved.

A cup? A bagatelle!

A permanent place in the annals of motoring? Not
even that.

For each of those drivers was an individual of charac-
ter—had to be, else how would he have gotten to this ad-
vanced stage over such a grueling course? And each of
those individual hearts beat with one all-consuming desire.

The late John Bunyan would have loved this situation.
As I walked through the wilderness of this world (he
would have said), I came upon a pleasure-ground by a
sparkling sea, the name of which was SIN. Here there
foregathered among a great multitude of people (who
were of the tribe known as ONLOOKERS) a score and
eight of pilgrims who had traveled to this place from the
corners of the earth to race the one with the other, and
the name of this race was LIFE.

There was one SIR CUTHBERT here, firm favorite among the bucks and the wiseacres, and as he sat there awaiting the Off with his esquire PERKINS, one lust and one lust only blazed within his breast, and this was the lust for *Power with Wealth*.

Nearby there sat another, straining at the leash with equal ardor, a southern peasant of dark aspect whose name was ANGELO. And beside him strained his companion of similar visage, one MARCELLO, and in spirit these two were as a single being interfused as by a blast of lightning with the lust known to men as *Escape from Routine*.

Then there came two who were square in the head and narrow of eye, the Teutons SCHICKEL and SCHWARTZ—and the prize for which they yearned was *Freedom with Riches*.

Next there came two of the English race, a military squire and his yeoman retainer, DAWLISH and BARRINGTON by name, and loath to offend though I may be, I will speak the truth, and speaking it, say that *Glory for the Motherland* may have been loose upon their lips, but what stirreth their hearts most lustily was *Free Publicity for the Squire's Inventions*. (On the petard of which, a starting device primed with gunpowder, they are hoist even as I record this matter—their carriage being blown in little pieces clean out of the race.)

And now comes one to whom few honest hearts will not warm, a bright-faced lad from the new Western Continent across the Atlantic Ocean, known to men as SCHOFIELD, but to the maiden who bends to wish him God's speed as CHESTER DARLING. And the prize and spur that pulls and goads him in this race is plain for everyone to see, and its name is *True Love*.

Moving a little farther along the line—

Doubtlessly Mr. Bunyan could have gone on like this without a pause, but since he has already touched upon the only competitors who concern us closely, and the starter's flag is already poised, we will leave the individual closeups for an overview of the circuit and the race itself. And for such a purpose, what better can be done than snatch another leaf or two from the screenwriter's book and give it as it might be presented in a multimillion-dollar production, complete with helicopter shots, the kind cooperation of a dozen motoring organizations, Mr. Schofield's wardrobe by Botany 500, Todd A-O, and color. But quickly now, because they're off. . . .

EXTERIOR. GRANDE CORNICHE. CÔTE D'AZUR, DAY.

The rally cars are spread out on the long road curving along the cliffside, high over the sea.

A series of HELICOPTER SHOTS, TRAVELING and FIXED, on the route show the progress of these cars.

SIR CUTHBERT, driving superbly, keeps his position ahead of the field.

MARCELLO and ANGELO, driving recklessly but brilliantly, overtake the car in front of them but still cannot catch CUTHBERT.

Behind them, SCHICKEL is driving the most spectacularly of all. He rounds hairpin bends with controlled skids which make one's toenails leap with one's heart to one's mouth, and he fearlessly overtakes where only millimeters come between him and a thousand-foot drop.

The MERCEDES becomes involved in a tremendous battle with the TRIPLE S. Side by side, they bump front wheels, and SCHICKEL looks at one time as if he will have to choose between falling behind the other car or over the edge of the cliff. But experience tells, and he manages to scrape past.

Then he draws level and almost passes the ITALIANS, but it is CUTHBERT who surprisingly always finds the necessary burst of speed to keep his distance as he zigzags up the hairpin bends.

Only once does disaster nearly befall the NIFTY NINE. When reaching the highest point, CUTHBERT meets a mule carrying logs. They slip from the animal's back just in front of the car. CUTHBERT swerves and nearly goes into the ravine. As the car bumps back onto the road, the new spare tire meets the fate of the last, flying out of its slot and bouncing over the edge of the road.

Below, and directly beneath it, races the LANCIA. The tire falls with a crash into the back seat.

CLOSE SHOT. INTERIOR LANCIA. TRAVELING.

The tire bursts open as it wedges itself between the front and back seats. MARCELLO swings around in alarm and sees jewelry pouring out of the tire.

ANGELO

Mamma mia! What's that?

MARCELLO

A tire! From heaven! (a beat)
It's-a full of jewels!

ANGELO

They musta be stolen. We gotta
do something.

MARCELLO

You crazy? We wanna win the rally.

RESUME SEQUENCE.

But the near-accident has been enough to cause AN-
GELO to slow down, and this gives SCHICKEL his op-
portunity to pass and speed ahead.

Meanwhile CHESTER is drawing closer to the ITAL-
IANS.

INTERIOR. TRIPLE S. TRAVELING.

CHESTER yawns, then glances at his watch. He looks
alarmed, then yawns again. Then he puts down his foot
and roars ahead.

RESUME SEQUENCE.

Now CHESTER begins to overtake the other. First
he passes the ITALIANS, then draws level with

SCHICKEL, and then with SIR CUTHBERT—whom he finally passes.

RESUME CLOSE SHOT. CHESTER. TRAVELING.

He looks over his shoulder and gives a triumphant sign to SIR CUTHBERT. But almost immediately he also gives a mighty yawn and starts to blink. He rubs his eyes, and the TRIPLE S begins to slow down.

RESUME SEQUENCE.

First CUTHBERT speeds ahead, then SCHICKEL, then the ITALIANS overtake CHESTER, and then the other cars. . . .

Gradually the TRIPLE S slows, until suddenly it veers off the road and comes to a stop behind some bushes.

CLOSE SHOT. CHESTER IN TRIPLE S. STATION-ARY.

He lays his head back on the driving seat, and with a beatific smile across his face, falls fast asleep. Judging from the noises issuing from his nose and lips, the car might just as well be renamed the TRIPLE Z.

ROAD TO MONTE CARLO.

The cars continue to race down toward the town, but it is the NIFTY NINE that comes roaring into the square to pass the checkered flag first.

Yes.

That's what it says here.

The Nifty Nine.

First.

And if Mr. Bunyan or anyone else were now to comment that at times in this world there would seem to be no justice whatsoever, we'd go along with him all the way.

CHAPTER 23

*The conclusion of this history, in which there will
be found, we trust, a little something for every-
body—including those who least deserve it.*

Pompous little twit and reveler in the limelight though he
was, Monsieur Dupont * was much like the rest of us
when it came to the really big public occasion: a bag of

*Dupont, Alphonse
b. Fontainebleau, 1882
f.   General Albert Napoléon Dupont
m. Giselle de Sarigney
ed. Lycée Lamouret, Sorbonne
married. Marie-Louise Sorbet, 2 daughters
military. Served in French Motorized Unit during the Great War,
        winning Croix de Guerre and attaining the rank of
        capitaine
address. c/o Automobile Club de Monaco, Automobile Club de
        France
clubs.   Automobile Club de Monaco, Automobile Club de
        France, Automobile Club de Nice, Royal Automobile
        Club de Grande Bretagne
hobbies. Automobiles
Note: In the absence of the official organizer for this year's
        Monte Carlo Rally, and of both the secretary and the
        assistant secretary of the Automobile Club de Monaco,
        Alphonse Dupont volunteered to take charge of the
        proceedings. In view of his great knowledge of motoring
        and of the rally itself (he won it at his second attempt),
        the offer was accepted.

nerves. And, much like many of us, his remedy for this was a few stiff brandies about half an hour before the event.

The event in this case was, of course, the presentation of the Coupe d'Honneur to the winner of the rally in the square outside the Hotel de Paris. This in itself involved a little extra bibbing, to be sure, for the cup was to be filled with champagne and the winner's health drunk by M. Dupont before being handed over. But that gentleman knew his capacity to the last dram, and in calculating the amount of brandy necessary if he was not to mar the occasion either by dithering like an old woman or offering brazenly to render the French equivalent of "Nelly Dean" or "Dear Old Pals," he had taken this extra swig or two into account. True, the rot might then set in pretty soon afterward, but by then the ceremony would be over and he could slur his words as much as he pleased.

It was therefore a bright-eyed but gaily confident Dupont who that day glanced around at the huge crowd, the journalists, the cameramen, and the local dignitaries, and lifted his hands for silence.

"It is my prerogative, my privilege, to present this magnificent Coupe d'Honneur to the man who, by his resoluteness, his unflagging courage, and his audacious driving, is the winner of this year's Monte Carlo Rally."

He picked up the brimming cup.

"Sir Cuthbert Ware-Armitage," he declaimed, addressing the winner (for, alas, nothing had happened since the race-off to alter that fact), "your health, *m'sieur*."

Whereupon Dupont took a long swig from the cup, decided he could risk it, held it to his lips for a further blissful liquid ten seconds, then handed it to Sir Cuthbert. Next he kissed the victor on both cheeks—which is no less than that stinker deserved—and placed the laurel wreath over Cuthbert's outrageously leering head. And if there are any among us sufficiently depraved to rejoice in the triumph of evil over good, they might as well rip out the remaining pages and call this

THE END

—unless, of course, like their despicable hero, their real pleasure is to hang around and savor their triumph and maybe kick a little dirt in the faces of the vanquished. They would? Very well, then. . . .

Sir Cuthbert beamed on the crowd, waved, bowed to Dupont, held up the cup, kissed it, and turned to Perkins, knowing full well that the latter would be hating every second of it.

"Well, I said we'd do it, Perkins, and we did!"

Somehow Perkins mustered a smile. Then, with a now-or-never glimmer of hope in his eyes, he leaned forward and whispered behind the cup: "Any chance of having my dossier back now, sir?"

Cuthbert looked at him—and even in that moment of glorious, total, and heady victory he hesitated, such was the basic badness of the man.

But there are limits to everything. And it would, after all, save him from paying the fellow any expected cash bonus.

He smiled.

"All right, you rascal," he said. "I'm a generous, soft-hearted, lovable old fool. Here you are. . . ."

And he held out the dossier, which, trembling with eagerness and relief, Perkins quickly took from him before disappearing into the crowd.

Nor was it a moment too soon.

For as Cuthbert raised the cup to his lips, an obviously

high-ranking officer of the local gendarmerie, accompanied by the Italian drivers, pushed their way through to him.

"Sir Cuthbert Ware-Armitage," said the officer, "may I have a word with you?"

His tone was not one of cheerful felicitation. Nor was it that of a man who seeks an autograph for a sick grandchild. But Cuthbert was too intoxicated with success to notice.

"Certainly, old *garçon*. But have a noggin of the bubbly first. Must look after the police, eh?"

The officer brushed aside the proffered cup. He held up a spare tire instead.

"Have you ever seen this tire before, sir?"

Cuthbert stared.

"Certainly not! Never seen it in my life!"

"Liar!" cried Marcello. "It fell out of your car into ours. I saw it with my own eyes!"

"You'lla be saying next you did not know it contained the Romanoff jewels," chimed in Angelo. "Don't think we are stupidos! We have had our eye on you ever since—alla time!"

Cuthbert gasped.

"I say! You're not suggesting I pinched this?"

"I think it would be better if you came with us to my headquarters," said the Frenchman.

"Quite unnecessary, officer," snapped Cuthbert. "I know *exactly* who stole that tire." He looked around. "Perkins!" he called.

Still holding the cup, he started to push his way through the crowd. Dupont grabbed a handle of the trophy but was pulled with it after Cuthbert, followed by the police officer and the two Italians.

"There you are!" cried Cuthbert, pointing to a corner of the flowerbeds across the square. "There's your man."

Perkins had been gleefully warming his hands at the small bonfire he'd made of the dossier. Now he looked up, startled, as the group bore down on him.

"Perkins," said Cuthbert, "tell these people how you got the tire last night."

The gendarme's uniform had not gone unnoticed by Perkins. He gulped and began to tremble. He stumbled to his feet.

"I—I—I—"

"Come along, Perkins! Be a man! These fellows say that the tire contained the Romanoff jewels. They've had the effrontery to say I pinched them. Tell them how we got the tire."

Perkins was silent now. His face was more than a mere picture. Rather was it like a movie screen—elongated vertically—which had been split up in the manner we have touched on earlier. The lower jaw, that is, still sagged, and the lips were still framing a vigorous denial, but in the right eye a look of indescribable cunning had appeared, while the upper-left portion of this PerkinScope screen was beginning to register pure vindictive, delirious joy.

He turned to the gendarme.

Without a blush, he made the following speech:

"It was like this, officer. He got it"—and here he nodded and looked Cuthbert full in the eye—"when we secretly switched cars, back there near Chambéry. The chap who brought the brand-new replacement fetched it with him. Sir Cuthbert gave him five thousand pounds for that tire. I thought it was rather expensive at the time."

Sir Cuthbert grabbed him by the tie. With foam-flecked lips, he howled:

"You liar! . . . Let me get at him!"

The gendarme and the Italians were dragging him off.

Then M. Dupont himself set up a howl, as he snatched back the Coupe d'Honneur.

"Cheat! Fraud! *Voleur!* He is worse than his father before him!"

He glared after Cuthbert. Then it was as if small fairy voices called, and he looked down to see that the remains of the champagne had been stirred into fresh activity by the treatment recently given to the cup. Without thinking, he lifted it to his lips and drained the lot.

"Excuse me. . . ."

He gave a guilty start, a faint burp, and then leered politely as he recognized the young English lady he'd ogled at more than once in the last few hours.

"Enchanted," he murmured, trying to clasp her by one of the four hands she appeared to be equipped with.

"Er—does this mean that all other competitors beat Sir Cuthbert?"

His face darkened at the very mention of that name.

"*Certainement!* So long as—hupp!—as they crosser finisher line."

And before he could suggest a little light supper back in his hotel that evening, she had thanked him with a charming smile and trotted off.

Reeling a little, he made his way back to the dais.

Already his assistants had brought along the next in line for the trophy—the Germans in their Mercedes. A cork popped even as Dupont arrived, and before he could say "Veuve Cliquot," into the cup sloshed another magnum of the Widow.

Dupont, undaunted, turned to the vastly increased crowd, waved grandly for silence, tottered a little, then addressed what looked like the two sets of twins in the Mercedes.

"Irris my prerogerrive, my *river*ledge, er presenn this mernificen Cou-hupp! d'Honneur, trer man who bize reslutions, zunflackerin curge anz dacious driving, isser winner this year's Mone Carlo Rally!"

He lifted the cup higher.

"Horse Muller froth Argentine," he cried, "your health, *m'sieur!*"

And he took a long long loving swig of the fresh cool liquid within. After which, with tears of brotherhood coursing down his cheeks, he leaned forward, and lurching and slobbering, kissed all the four happy faces he could see before him, on both cheeks of each, making in all eight kisses (though some fell on empty air, you understand).

It was a happy scene, if a trifle messy.

Now, there are no doubt some among us who, perhaps being themselves of German origin, would like to call it a day here, feeling that the victory, thus revised, is only as it should be. After all, Schickel and Schwartz may have been crooks. Their original purpose may have been nefarious. But in the context of the rally itself their adherence to its principal rules had been strict and their general conduct, if not impeccable, then at least as good as anyone else's.

Very well. We have no basic quarrel with either of them. We are even prepared to grant that poor upbringing had probably been the cause of their later delinquencies, and that had they been given their rightful quota of candy, kittens, and comic books as kids they would both have become highly respected members of the community.

So go ahead. We are not intolerant of minorities. We respect the civil rights of others. Just go right ahead, take scissors to the rest of this chapter if you want—and call this

THE END

—unless, of course, you want to hang around while these two reformed characters sell the cup and give the proceeds to the local poor—in which case you're in for a pretty long wait. For just then up stepped another brace of gendarmes.

Otto sighed. That look on those faces—he knew it of old.

"*Auf wiedersehen*, Horst Muller!" he groaned.

His companion nodded. But being made of sterner stuff, he snatched off his false moustache, turned to the cameraman, and said with veritable Beethovenian defiance: "Quick! A photograph of Willi Schickel!"

That being done, the two men relaxed and smiled as the bracelets were fastened on their helpfully outstretched wrists. Then off they went to assist the police with their inquiries, while Dupont recovered and ordered the cup to be recharged and the next in line to be brought along.

These were Angelo and Marcello.

Dupont nodded at them gravely.

"You are both of age? You are not likely to be arrested?"

These remarks struck him as being so witty that he suddenly started giggling—and all the iron control he'd been exerting in the past few minutes melted like butter in the sun.

Then he held up his hands, all sixteen of them, and there was silence.

The speech he made then is practically unrecordable. Basically it was the same as the one he'd made to the others, but it was punctuated with so many hicks and burps and peals of sardonic laughter—and interrupted by so many observations on life and the law and the strange workings of the criminal mind—to say nothing of old Provençal saws, Napoleonic maxims, and the wit and wisdom of an elderly female relative of M. Dupont's—that the reporters present flung away their pencils in disgust.

It came to an end, however, as all ordeals must, to be followed by much passing and snatching and recapturing of the cup as it danced between the fifty-four hands and twenty-seven mouths of Dupont and the two Italians, and this in turn came to an end with the arrival of Marie-Claude and her two companions. Whereupon M. Dupont burst into tears and made a speech, if anything, rather more incomprehensible than the last, in which he declared he'd behaved like a pig to the French girls, a pig, a misogynistic brute (which he had, obstructing them at every turn), and could they ever find it in their hearts to take pity on him and lighten his declining years by bestowing upon him their forgiveness (which was no sooner said than done). Then the Italians put the French girls' hands on the cup, and they all began hugging and kissing one another, and M. Dupont passed out, and the crowd applauded, and a greater cheer than ever went up, and everyone turned in time to see:

The Triple S. It was approaching the finishing line. Chester was fast asleep at the wheel, but Betty was walking alongside the car and doing the steering while a mob of urchins pushed it from behind.

And as they crossed the line, such a cheer went up that it was said to have been heard as far away as Nice, and it woke Chester up.

"Yankee doodle dandies!" he gasped. "Whatever happened?"

"You've done it, Chester! You may not have won the rally—"

(Italian readers may uncross their fingers and leave us here, if they wish, for what Betty said was perfectly true . . .

FINE

. . . there you are—*arrivederci*, and love to Maria and the kids.)

"—but you've beaten old Cuthbert and won the bet!" continued Betty.

Chester flung out his arms.

"Whoopee! Now we can be married!"

"Yes, oh, yes!" gasped Betty, falling into those arms. "And here's the man who's agreed to marry us. He got here just this morning."

Chester screwed up his eyes, trying to focus the approaching figure. Betty reached into his pocket and took out his glasses.

"Here!" She laughed. "And don't let's have any more nonsense about these." She stuck them on his nose and said: "Meet my darling Grandpapa!"

The figure came into focus. Chester gave a start.

For there was no doubt about the old man's relationship to Cuthbert. His hair was white and his upper lip clean-shaven, but the contours were exactly the same, even unto the frontal gap in the top teeth.

"How do you do, young man?" the bishop smiled. "I say, wasn't it awfully bad luck about poor old Cuthbert?" he added as Chester shook his hand.

But his grin broadened even as he said it, and there was something about its slow spread that was so uncannily reminiscent of Cuthbert himself that from that moment on Chester never had any difficulty in believing that the old boy could have done anything so wicked as to give a blackmailer a hold over him.

Indeed, that probably accounts for the fact that although the firm of Armitage Motors passed completely into Chester's and Betty's control—much to the relief of the company secretary—Cuthbert came out of it with what he grudgingly termed "a small but not inadequate pension for life."

THE END

—and this time it really is.